COTTAGE NEAR
THE POINT

KAY CORRELL

ROSE QUARTZ PRESS

This book is dedicated to all my readers. I'm so grateful for each and every one of you.

KAY'S BOOKS

Find more information on all my books at
kaycorrell.com

COMFORT CROSSING ~ THE SERIES
The Shop on Main - Book One
The Memory Box - Book Two
The Christmas Cottage - A Holiday Novella
(Book 2.5)
The Letter - Book Three
The Christmas Scarf - A Holiday Novella
(Book 3.5)
The Magnolia Cafe - Book Four
The Unexpected Wedding - Book Five

The Wedding in the Grove - (a crossover short story

between series - with Josephine and Paul from The Letter.)

LIGHTHOUSE POINT ~ THE SERIES
Wish Upon a Shell - Book One
Wedding on the Beach - Book Two
Love at the Lighthouse - Book Three
Cottage near the Point - Book Four
Return to the Island - Book Five

INDIGO BAY ~ A multi-author sweet romance series
Sweet Sunrise - Book Three
Sweet Holiday Memories - A short holiday story
Sweet Starlight - Book Nine

Sign up for my newsletter at my website *kaycorrell.com* to make sure you don't miss any new releases or sales.

CHAPTER 1

She really should stay at the Hamilton Hotel in Sarasota. That's what she'd told her father. It was closer to her client. It was logical. But for some reason Samantha Thompson couldn't quite understand, she found herself crossing the bridge to Belle Island instead.

She'd rolled down the windows on her rental car and let the crisp, salty air flow through the vehicle. Her hair flew in a million directions and for a brief moment, she felt that old rush of excitement. The same feeling she'd had every summer crossing this bridge for her yearly stay on the island.

But nothing was the same now. Nothing.

Her mood deflated as quickly as it had swept over her. Maybe this wasn't such a good idea. She crossed the bridge and rolled onto the island. The same lazy, old-Florida atmosphere pervaded the town, and she was glad of that. No high rises. Not a fast food chain in sight.

She drove to the office of Island Property Management and parked her car. The woman she'd spoken to earlier had assured her they had the perfect beach cottage rental for her. She retrieved the key and directions from the friendly and efficient woman working in the office and headed off to Gulf Avenue to find the rental.

Once again, her car had a mind of its own, and she found herself parking by Lighthouse Point before heading to the cottage. She sat in the car staring out at the point. Waves of memories crashed over her. She slowly pushed open the door and slid out, sucked into a swirling vortex of joy mixed with dread.

She simply wanted to walk out on the beach.

Feel the sand beneath her feet.

Feel the breeze caress her skin.

Soak in the sun.

She'd only stay a minute. That's all.

Samantha Thompson stood at the edge of the beach

at Lighthouse Point. The lighthouse rose up beside her on the land jutting out into the sea, a lone protector, towering over the beach. She smiled at the familiar sight and, like a young child, raced onto the expansive white sand. It had been far too long. The sun bathed over her and she laughed out loud as she spun around in the cool sea breeze. She took a quick look around to see if anyone was watching her craziness, but there was just one old couple walking hand in hand way down the beach. *Perfect*. She spun around in circles again, arms out wide.

A mild dizziness swept over her and she quit her antics. She shook her head at her silliness and walked to the water's edge. Samantha stood at the edge of the ocean, watching the sun twinkle and blink on the waves. She took a few steps back, out of the reach of the gentle waves, and sank down onto the beach. Her hands skimmed over the sand and she picked up a seashell, turning it slowly over and over on her palm.

The magic of Lighthouse Point. She didn't really believe in the fairy tale now, but she sure had as a young girl. It was just silly town folklore, she knew that now.

It all started when one of the first settlers to the town had lost her sea-faring husband at sea. The woman had gone to the end of Lighthouse Point and wished for her husband to return. She'd carefully thrown a shell into the ocean as she made her wish. Three months later, to the day, her husband had returned to her. He'd been rescued by another ship and travelled back to the island. The town lore proclaimed if someone walked to the end of Lighthouse Point, made a wish, and tossed a shell into the ocean, their wish would come true.

How many times had she done that as a young girl?

Too many to count. So many wishes. Some small, foolish ones, some big ones. Always wishing…

She sighed. Why had she stayed away from Lighthouse Point for all these years? The southern Florida town had been her whole life every summer when she was growing up. She and her mother would come and stay with her grandparents at their beach house. Her father traveled all the time for business anyway, so there was no need to stay in the Midwest after school was out each year. Her father would try and make it down to see them once a month or so, but they'd never counted on it.

The summers had been glorious days of sunshine, swimming in the ocean, collecting shells and so, so many memories of her grandparents.

Then everything had changed the summer she turned sixteen. Nothing in her life had ever been the same since then.

Harry Moorehouse pulled his truck into a parking space on Oak Street. The truck shuddered to a stop and he shook his head, hoping the old girl would keep herself together long enough for him to find a reasonably priced replacement for her. Belle Island was bustling with activity today in the late January busy season. The island was awash with snow birds hiding out from the harsh winter up north. He loved this time of year in southern Florida. The weather was mild, sometimes even a bit cold, not beastly hot and humid like in the summertime.

He climbed out of the truck and crossed over to his office. A sign—which he still thought had cost too much—proclaimed the office of Island Property Management. He wasn't even sure how he'd gotten to this point. First he'd agreed to watch Miss Melanie's rental house for her when she'd moved to Jackson to be near her daughter and grandkids. Then Mr. Sullivan had asked if he wanted to manage a small resort property with six units in it. Next thing he knew, he was managing a whole handful of rental properties. He'd hired a crew of maintenance workers and an accountant to handle the leasing monies. A few years ago he'd bought this property on Oak Street and it officially became Island Property Management. He still couldn't believe he owned his own company, a thriving one at that.

So he should be able to buy a new truck, right? But old habits die hard. Even though he needed a reliable truck for the business, he wasn't used to spending money on himself. He promised himself that he'd go to the mainland, drive to Sarasota, and look for a new truck. Well, maybe a used truck that was in good condition…

He pushed through the door and Lisa, his receptionist—assistant—right-hand person—smiled up at him. She flashed him the just a minute sign as she finished up on the phone.

"Hey, Harry."

"How's it going?" Harry picked up the stack of mail on Lisa's desk. She'd carefully sorted everything and placed the items he needed to see in his basket. She was an organizational angel.

"Cable is out in unit four at Point Breeze. Again. I'll get ahold of Mac and have him head over." Lisa finished jotting down a note. "Oh, and we got a week's rental for the Sea Haven cottage to fill that last-minute vacancy."

"Good. How about the repairs to the Jensen's cottage from that bachelor party gone wild?"

"Had to put down new carpet and the now married not-so-bachelor is not amused that he's being charged for the expense. Not sure how he thought we could repair scorched carpeting..."

"He's lucky he and his buddies didn't burn the whole place down." Harry shook his head. "I don't understand people sometimes."

"The Big House is totally rented for the summer season now. The cancellation in June got filled."

Harry smiled at Lisa's reference to The Big House. That's what they called this monstrosity of a house near the end of the point. Ten bedrooms, eight baths, and just huge. For obvious reasons Lisa had nicknamed it The Big House and the name had stuck, though they did list it for rent on their website under the owner's preferred name of "The Great Escape."

"Okay, good. I'll be in my office if you need me."

Harry crossed over to a small office in the back of the building. He dropped his stack of paperwork onto the old wooden desk and sank into the worn leather chair. The sun filtered through the blinds on the window, throwing slants of light across his desk. Maybe if he put his mind to it, he could finish up his work and still have time to go for a brisk walk on the beach late afternoon. With the image dangling firmly in his mind, he tackled the first paper in the stack.

Lisa stuck her head in the door a while later. "Can you swing by the Sea Haven cottage on your way home? The renter called and said there's a small leak under the kitchen sink. She put a pot under there, but I figured you'd want to check it out. I thought you could look at it on your way home since it's right down from where you're staying and fixing up Bellemire Cottage."

"No problem." Didn't look like he was going to get that late afternoon walk in today after all.

CHAPTER 2

Samantha sat on the small deck of Sweet Haven, the cottage she'd rented for the week. How she would have loved to stay at her grandparents' beach house, but it had been sold long ago. The house she'd rented was a few cottages down from her grandparents' old home. The rental cottage used to be owned by the Masons, back when she was a little girl. She didn't remember much about them, except that they'd been an old, retired couple and friends with her grandparents. She'd been in their cottage back then, but it didn't look the same now. Someone had rehabbed it with a new kitchen, fancy bathrooms, and tile floor throughout. A new wall of windows had been installed on the ocean side, with spectacular views of the sea.

She sat staring out at the waves, mesmerized by their flowing motion. The wind had calmed down some as the afternoon wore on, and the waves gently rolled onto the beach. How many hours had she sat on this same beach, watching the waves?

Until… she hadn't.

"Hello?"

The voice called from the side of the house. The rental agency. She'd forgotten they said they'd come by and fix the leak. She couldn't hear the doorbell from out on the deck and a person soon learned to come around to the seaside if someone didn't answer the front door. A tall, dark-haired man came around the corner of the house and up the few stairs of the deck.

"Ma'am, I came here to—" The man lifted his head up and looked directly at her. "Sammy."

Samantha glanced at the man staring at her. He looked familiar, and yet it was his voice that confirmed it. "Harry."

There was a part of her that wanted to launch into his arms, for the years to fade away, but that wasn't going to happen. She wasn't a young girl with her summer crush on the cutest boy in town.

Anyway, not after what had happened all those years ago.

She tried to think of the words to say, but they were stuck in her throat, behind the distant memories and suppressed feelings of hurt and shame.

Harry didn't appear to be doing any better than she was with his deer-in-the-headlights look.

"How did you know I was here?" Her voice was barely more than a whisper.

"I didn't… I mean, I came to fix…"

Samantha finally processed her thoughts. "You work for the rental company?" Harry had always been a handy guy, tinkering with things, fixing them.

"I…" He looked at her for a long moment. "Yes, I came to look at the leak. May I?" He nodded toward the inside of the cottage.

"Of course, go on in." She wondered if she should follow him inside, but she sat in the Adirondack chair, quiet in her indecision. After all these years, did they have nothing to say to each other?

How have you been? It's great to see you. But she'd said none of those words out loud.

She finally decided she should go inside—what was she afraid of, anyway? But as she pushed out of the chair, Harry came striding out the door into the late afternoon sunshine.

"All fixed."

Silence. Again.

She took a deep breath. "You always could fix just about anything."

He looked at her, a slow gaze from the top of her head to her pink painted toenails in her absurd, loud-colored flip flops. It was probably a bit chilly to be wearing flip flops in January, but she hadn't been able to resist. She'd been wearing snow boots when she left Chicago. "You look good, Sams."

Her heart hammered in her chest. He looked better than good. Tall, in need of a bit of a shave. His thick brown hair was cut short. His thin boyhood frame had turned into a man's body with broad shoulders tapering down to a lean waist. He wore a pale blue, short-sleeved knit shirt with Island Property Management embroidered on it. The shirt only served to brighten the color of his sea-blue eyes. Worn jeans—but not too worn— covered his long legs. He'd had quite the growth spurt since she'd last seen him. She'd guess her head would just barely come up to his chin now.

She collected her thoughts enough to answer him. "Uh, thanks." What a gracious answer to a compliment. She wanted to roll her eyes at herself.

Was that even possible?

Grams would be so proud of how well she'd imparted her manner lessons…

"It's been a lot of years, hasn't it?"

"A lot." Twenty years, to be exact. Not that she wanted *him* to know she knew exactly how long it had been.

"It's been twenty years, Sammy."

That stunned her to silence. He knew, too. Exactly.

"I wish…" Harry paused and looked out at the ocean. "Remember all those summers? I used to live for the months when you and your mom would come to Belle Island. We practically grew up together. I remember the first time I met you. I think you were about eight or so. You had your hair in braids, skinned knees, and you were carrying the heaviest pail of seashells, struggling to cart it back to your grandmother's."

"You wanted to carry the bucket for me."

"I did. But you said no. You said you didn't need a stinkin' boy to carry your shells."

Harry smiled at her then. *That smile.* The one she remembered. The one that still took her breath away and made her heart beat at a ridiculous speed all at the same time.

"Luckily I won you over later that summer with my charm and wit." Harry winked at her.

"I looked forward to my summers here, too." She had. Every year on the last day of school she'd raced home to pack for the summer and nag her mother that they should get on the road to Florida.

"Until you didn't come back." Harry's face went from playful teasing to a sad, haunted look.

"It was a long time ago." Samantha fought back her own emotions.

"It was." Harry stared at her again, then rubbed a hand over his face as if to make sure he was really seeing her. "So, why are you back on Belle Island?"

"I... I'm working in Sarasota. Have a client there. I probably should have stayed there in town, but... well, I wanted to see the island again."

She could hear Harry suck in a deep breath. "So..." He paused. "Maybe we could grab dinner or something and catch up?"

"Uh, maybe." Samantha wasn't sure it was a good idea, but at that exact same moment, she knew she wouldn't be able to stay away from him now that she knew he was here, too. "Sure. Okay."

Harry smiled at her again, a boyish look of expectation crossing his face. "Tomorrow at Magic Cafe? I'll pick you up and we'll walk down the beach. Six-ish?"

"Magic Cafe is still here? Do they still have the best hush puppies? Oh, and blackened grouper. I want grouper." She clapped her hands in delight.

Harry laughed. "Yes, they do. And ice cold beer if you're of the beer drinking sort. I'll see you at six." He turned and clomped down the wooded stairs of the deck. He turned when he reached the sand. "It's really great to see you again." With a small wave, he headed around the corner of the cottage.

Well, the day was full of surprises. First she'd agonized over her decision to come to Belle Island. She liked to think each decision through from every angle to make sure she wasn't making a mistake.

At least *now* she did that. She'd learned her lesson on not thinking things through.

But the urge to come to the island when she would be this close had overcome her cautious nature and she'd booked the cottage.

Then Harry had shown up. She thought he would have been long gone from town. She'd always had the sense that he felt he hadn't truly fit in here on the island. But here he was doing maintenance for a rental agency in town.

She wasn't sure she liked the stream of surprises that had pummeled her today.

~

Harry slammed the door to the truck and coaxed the engine to life. He pulled out of the drive of Sea Haven cottage with a swish of sand trailing behind him. His heart pounded in his chest and he swallowed.

Then swallowed again.

He'd thought he would never see Sammy again. But here she was, twenty years later. She'd become a beautiful woman. While the friendship years when they were young had become a teenage crush the last few summers she'd come to Belle Island, none of that had compared to the punch in the gut he'd gotten this afternoon when he'd climbed those stairs and looked into her whiskey-colored eyes.

He pulled into the sandy drive in front of the cottage he was staying at and leaned his forehead against the steering wheel, trying to catch his breath. Flashes of memories swam in his head. Sammy as a young girl, trying to act brave after being stung by a jellyfish. Sammy laughing as she told him stories about her life at her fancy private girls' school in Chicago. The way her face looked so serious when, every year at the end of the summer, they'd go to Lighthouse Point and make their wish that everything would stay the same when she came back the next summer. Until that last summer. They'd made their wish and slowly walked away, down the beach, holding hands. Then that very afternoon everything changed, and he never saw her or heard from her again.

Harry got out of the truck and went inside the cottage. He'd been staying here for months, working on renovations for it in the evenings or when work didn't keep him tied to the office. While he often stayed in rental properties and rehabbed them for the owners, drifting from condo to cottage, this project was special. He wanted to repay a debt he owed. Then maybe, just maybe, he would find some peace.

He peered into the fridge, snagged a bottle of beer, grabbed his toolbox, and headed outside. He was almost finished with the new deck. He probably had a good hour or so of daylight left, so he got to work on the railing. This weekend he hoped to finish the benches he was making to line the deck for extra seating. He worked for an hour, pausing to watch the sun set in an explosion of orange and pink.

How many sunsets had he watched with Sammy? She loved sunsets and would pause whatever they were doing to race to get a view of the sunset, sometimes sitting quietly in awe, sometimes exclaiming out loud at the kaleidoscope of colors. Occasionally she'd spin around on the beach, arms out wide, the colors of the sunset wrapping around her while she danced on the beach. He smiled at the memory.

He watched the last of the sun slip below the horizon, ending the day. He sat on a deck chair watching the night creep in and the first stars come out to blink in the sky. He remained there, silent, lost in memories of warm summer nights gone by.

CHAPTER 3

Harry took a quick look in the mirror, straightened the collar on his shirt, then headed out to the beach to walk to the cottage where Sammy was staying. He ambled to the edge of the surf, just out of reach of the water. He loved how Belle Island had a handful of restaurants scattered along the beach so you could just walk up to them. No dodging traffic and no fighting for a parking space in the busy season, just walk down the beach and grab a meal. Magic Cafe was definitely his favorite place to eat in town. He wasn't sure how much of that was because of the millions of times he'd gone there with Sammy when they were kids. He'd socked away a couple dollars here, a few more dollars there. Taken odd jobs around town. He'd saved up money all year long so he could take Sammy on a couple of real dates each summer.

Or maybe he loved the restaurant because of Tally. She'd owned the Magic Cafe since as far back as he could remember. When he'd been a teenager, scrambling for jobs, Tally had always managed to find something that needed fixing at her restaurant or her house. He wasn't sure everything actually needed to be fixed, but he'd appreciated the extra work back then. She'd always managed to find him a plate of what she said were "leftovers" when he'd gone there to work. Wages and a hot meal, the perfect duo as far as he'd been concerned.

He continued his walk down the beach, careful to not let the waves splash up on his slacks. Within a few minutes he was at the cottage where Sammy was staying. She was waiting for him out on the deck and she raised her hand in greeting. He crossed from the water's edge up to her deck.

"Hey, Harry."

"Hi. You ready to go?" Why hadn't he thought to bring her flowers? She loved flowers. He should have remembered that and brought some. Maybe as... a peace offering?

Sammy smiled at him. "I am. Can't wait to go back to the Magic Cafe. I have to admit, I had to keep myself from going there for lunch. I went to a place called The Sweet Shoppe."

"That's owned by Julie Farmington. She used to work for Tally at Magic Cafe, but then opened up her own bakery and cafe."

"It was delicious. They had the best fresh-baked sandwich bread."

"Yes, it's a good place to grab a sandwich, but you should try it for breakfast. Julie outdoes herself on breakfast pastries."

"I'll have to try that." Sammy stepped down onto the beach. "After lunch I wandered around town for a bit. Found a cute gift shop. I admit to buying a darling Lighthouse Point t-shirt." Sammy grinned. "Pink, of course."

"Of course. I see that's still your favorite color." Harry eyed her khaki slacks, crisp white shirt, and shocking-pink sweater.

Sammy laughed. "Yes, it's still my favorite." She whirled around showing off her sweater.

"Still lookin' fine."

"Why, thank you, sir." She grabbed his hand and tugged him towards the ocean. "Let's walk at the water's edge, okay?"

He let her lead him down to the water. To be honest, right now he'd let her lead him just about anywhere in the world, without one word of complaint. About halfway to the water she dropped his hand and raced ahead of him. The wind whipped her hair in wild abandon and she swirled in circles, her arms open wide, as she reached the surf. Oh, he remembered that so well. Her whirling and swirling. The sound of her laughter trickled across the beach, and he trotted down to the water.

The wind tossed her long brown hair this way and that, the curls tangling up in a mass of gorgeous chestnut locks. She laughed again, and snatched her curls back with one hand, entrapping them in an impromptu ponytail to keep them out of her eyes.

He stood staring at her like a fool.

Harry stared at her with a look of *what* in his eyes? He probably thought she was a crazy person twirling around on the sand. She just couldn't help herself. She loved the beach. It was like the sea filled her whole soul with joy, flooding her with happy thoughts, and making her feel so alive. More alive than she'd felt in twenty years. How in the world had she let herself stay away this long?

"Quit staring." Sammy stopped long enough to give Harry a no-nonsense glare.

"I wasn't...well, I was. I couldn't help it. You

looked just like that free-spirited girl I knew so long ago."

And with that one sentence the wind was knocked out of her sails. She wasn't that girl anymore. She was a grown woman, for Pete's sake. With responsibilities. Things that needed to be accomplished. Goals to reach. She was such a goal setter now. Life goals, ten year goals, five year goals, goals for this year.

She slowly started to walk toward Magic Cafe. The evening sun glowed around them as they strolled along the shore, not talking, but comfortable in their silence. When they got to the cafe, they crossed the beach and went up the stairs at the entrance.

"Harry. Good to see you." Tally greeted them with a stack of menus in her hands. "Wait. Is that Sammy Thompson?" Tally's eyes widened. "It *is* you."

Tally enveloped her in a warm embrace. "Oh my word. It is so good to see you. I'd have known you anywhere. You've grown into a beautiful woman, hon."

A deluge of emotions and memories stormed down on Sammy. Hot summer days. Warm summer nights. The smell of fried fish. The luscious taste of her first bite of a hush puppy each summer.

"It's so good to see you, too." Sammy hugged the woman. Tally smelled of fresh air, fried foods, and the faint hint of suntan lotion.

"You kids come and sit down. You want to sit outside, right? I'll get you a table right by the beach with a nice view of the ocean. We'll turn on the overhead heaters if it gets too chilly." Tally threaded her way through the tables and placed the menu on a two-top wooden table. "I'll send Tereza over to take your order. I'll be back and check on you in a while."

Harry pulled out her chair, and Sammy slipped into it. The familiar site of the plastic-covered menu made her smile. It hadn't changed much at all in the years she'd been away. In the summer, ceiling fans stirred the air from overhead. In chilly weather, heaters tossed down their warmth on the outside eating area. Tables were also scattered around the edge of the covered deck, with umbrellas shading the customers from the sun during the day. Down near the water's edge, a group of children ran back and forth on the shore, laughing.

"What are you smiling about?"

"The menu. The view. Tally. It is all so familiar. I've missed this place. All of Belle Island, actually." She'd even missed Harry, not that she'd realized it until this very moment. Or maybe it was that she'd never let herself miss him.

"Well, we're glad to have you back." Harry lifted the menu, looked at it, then laughed. "There really is no need for me to look at it. I already know what I'm having. A matter of fact, I bet I know what you're having. A blackened grouper sandwich, hush puppies and... a beer? You a beer drinker now?"

"I am. A Corona with lime sounds good."

Their waitress came up to them, her pen poised over a worn order pad. "Hi, I'm Tereza. What can I get you?" Her voice held the faint trace of a Greek accent.

"Hey, Tereza. You new here? I don't think I've seen you before." Harry smiled at the waitress.

"I moved here a month or so ago. I was lucky enough to get this job with Tally. I really like it here. I live right over on the mainland."

"Well, welcome to the area." Harry still had his friendly smile on his face, and for the briefest moment Sammy was jealous. That was crazy, right?

Harry was oblivious to her zigzagging emotions.

"We'll have two Coronas. And we'll each have the blackened grouper sandwich and hush puppies." Harry looked at Sammy. "Do you want a salad with that?"

"No. I don't think so."

"That will be it then." Harry took her menu and handed both of them to Tereza. He leaned back and stretched his long legs under the table. They bumped up against her leg, but she didn't move away. She liked the small connection to him.

"So, you're working for the rental company?" She wanted to know what this older Harry was like.

"Um…yes." Harry shifted in his chair. "What do you do?"

"I work for my father's advertising company. I'm actually the CEO now. We're trying to land a new client in Sarasota, Adriana Boutiques. That's why I'm here."

"Do you work crazy long hours like he always did?"

"Usually."

Silence fell between them. Neither wanted to ask the obvious question that hung between them. The question that had haunted her for twenty years. Neither one wanted to talk about her mother…

So they didn't.

Sammy and Harry walked across the sand and down to the ocean. Night had fallen and Harry waited for his eyes to adjust from the brighter lights of the cafe to the filtered moonlight on the beach. It was a clear night, with an almost full moon that helped light their way.

"That was so good. I'd forgotten how delicious that grouper sandwich was. I ate way too much." Sammy led the way down the soft sand. "Though, I could probably be convinced to go back there again tomorrow."

"Are you asking me on a date?" Harry teased.

"I. Well. I don't know. Do you want to go on a date with me?"

"I'm thinking tonight qualified as one, didn't it?"

"I thought it was more just old friends getting together." Sammy looked at him, her eyes questioning.

"Okay, then. That settles it. We'll have to go out again to have our first official date. Well, first date since you returned to the island." He took her hand in his and they walked quietly down the beach. The salty evening air had a hint of a nip to it. It was a perfect night for a beach stroll. Or maybe it was perfect because Sammy's hand was in his once again after all these years.

A small sigh escaped Sammy's lips.

"I heard that." Harry squeezed her hand.

"It's just nice to be back. I wish I wouldn't have stayed away so long."

"I wish you wouldn't have, either."

"I couldn't face coming back. Everything fell apart that night. It was the beginning of the end for my family."

"I know it was. I wish I could have taken it back. Made it all go away."

"But it *did* happen and nothing has ever been the same." A tormented expression covered her face.

"I'm so sorry, Sammy."

"Well, it wasn't your fault."

"I'm still sorry it happened."

They walked on in silence until they reached Sweet Haven, and he led her up the steps to the deck. "Want to sit for a bit?"

Sammy nodded and dropped onto one of the Adirondack chairs facing the ocean. He slipped into one beside her, staring out at the sea. An awkward silence crackled between them. Finally, she turned and looked at him. He was glad to see the haunted look had eased, and she gave him a tiny smile. "It was nice catching up with you again, Harry." She swept her hair away from her face and let out a long breath. "But, it's getting late. I better go inside." With that, she stood and slipped into the cottage.

He continued to sit on the chair, lost in

memories. He didn't think anything that had happened that night, so many years ago, was Sammy's fault... but he understood her feeling that way. Sometimes the choices you make have unintended consequences. He understood that, too.

CHAPTER 4

The next day Sammy got up early and brewed herself a pot of coffee—one of her vices—and took a steaming cup out to the deck. She sat on the deck chairs and watched the world come alive. The seagulls swooped overhead, calling their friends. The sandpipers danced in the foamy remains of the waves. A few joggers ran past, headphones on, missing the sounds of the early morning. But then, she shouldn't feel sorry for them, they were getting their exercise. Unlike her, sitting on her deck, just watching.

After two cups of coffee, she was awake enough to start her day. A quick shower, jeans, and a light sweater, and she was ready to go.

Only she didn't know what to do with her day. Her client had called to reschedule their appointment for tomorrow. She'd done her research and perfected her presentation. She just needed to cool her heels until tomorrow, and cooling her heels was definitely not her strong suit.

Suddenly, she knew what she wanted to do. *Needed* to do. She slipped out to the beach and walked slowly down the sand, drawn to her grandparent's cottage, Bellemire. She wanted to see it again. Needed to.

The cottage had been freshly painted a soothing mint green. Fresh wood proclaimed that someone was putting on a new deck. One lone chair sat on it.

She walked around to the front door and knocked, not knowing what she'd say if someone answered. No one did, so she looked both directions and stealthily walked back to the deck and slowly climbed the steps. She peered inside through the French doors where the window coverings weren't fully closed. In the dimly lit cottage she could see large boxes stacked in the main area.

She stepped back, feeling only *slightly* guilty for trespassing. She trailed her hand along the siding, as if trying to connect to her past. She stood on the deck and gazed at the glorious, sun-filled view, just like she had so, so many times before.

She looked up at a lone blue heron flapping its lazy way down the beach, and an idea began to form.

She knew what she could do. It wouldn't make everything right, it wouldn't change the mess she'd made out of her family, but at least it might ease her guilt.

She was going to try and buy back her grandparents' cottage.

At lunchtime, Harry hurried into the Lucky Duck to meet Jamie. He'd finally convinced his friend to take a quick break from running the inn he owned with his mother. His friend had recently gotten married, too, so between the inn and his new wife, Jamie was a busy man.

Harry slid onto a barstool. "Sorry I'm late. Got tied up with yet another problem at the Jensen's place."

"The rental that had that wild bachelor party?" Jamie set down his large glass of sweet tea.

"That very one." Harry motioned to Willie, the bartender, and pointed to Jamie's tea. Will nodded and poured another brimming glass.

"Hey, Harry. Here you go." Willie set the glass in front of him. "What can I get you two to eat?"

"Burger and fries for me." Jamie looked at Harry.

"Same for me."

"Coming right up." Willie left to turn in their order.

Harry turned to Jamie. "You'll never believe who's back in town."

"Who?"

"Sammy Thompson."

Jamie's eyes widened. "Sammy from when we were kids? That Sammy? The one who just up and disappeared on you?"

"That very one."

"What's she doing back in town?"

"She's working in Sarasota, but decided to stay here on the island." Harry took a swig of his tea. "We actually went out last night to Magic Cafe."

"No kidding."

"And… we talked about going out again."

"You sure you know what you're doing?" Jamie raised an eyebrow.

"Possibly not." Harry raked a hand through his hair. "*Probably* not. But it seems I can't help myself. When I saw her it was like… like I was that kid again. You remember that kid. The one who couldn't get enough time with her every summer."

"I do remember that boy."

"Well, it seems the grown-up version of that kid still can't keep away from her." Harry sighed. "I'm a very weak male, what can I say?"

Jamie laughed. "Well, don't make me pick up the pieces again when she leaves."

"Nah, that won't happen." He was a grown man now and knew how to protect his heart. Right?

Sammy sat at her computer and did her search engine magic. It appeared Bellemire had been resold multiple times since her grandparents had owned it. There was evidence that it had been rental property off and on with various owners. She wondered what kind of shape the cottage was in now and what was in all those boxes. Was someone moving out? Moving in?

Before long she'd located a real estate agent and had an appointment for that very afternoon. Her father would probably be furious, but she'd cross that bridge when she came to it. She needed time to see if she could make everything work. She hoped the agent could help her purchase her grandparents' cottage, even though it wasn't technically on the market. She'd make a really, really good offer they wouldn't want to refuse. It would be worth it if she could finally make things right.

Later that afternoon, she drove down Gulf Avenue, the road that ran behind all the houses on the beach, and turned onto the main road, Seaside Boulevard—which was a misnomer because it ran the length of the island straight down the middle. Not a glimpse of the sea was visible from it. The town had put in numerous parking lots right off of Seaside Boulevard since she'd last been here, probably in response to their increase in tourism. The town had really grown in twenty years, which wasn't that surprising. They'd done a good job at keeping the same old Florida vibe with the town though. They'd limited buildings to two stories plus those stilt things—she couldn't think of what they were called— some of the homes by the ocean were built on. She found the real estate office and pulled her car into a nearby parking spot.

Her agent, Jane Munson, was a petite woman with boundless energy. She motioned for Sammy to have a seat, while handing her a bottle of water and juggling a stack of papers.

"So, you're looking for beach property on Belle Island."

"I am. A particular cottage." She gave Jane the address.

Jane sat on the edge of her chair and clicked the keys on her computer.

"Ah, yes. I've found the property you're interested in. It's not on the market though, you know that, right?"

"I do. But I'm interested in contacting the owners to see if they are willing to sell."

"I can do that, but the property is listed in the name of a trust. I'll have to do some digging around and see if I can find some more information to see how to contact the owners."

"I'd appreciate that."

"It hopefully won't take too long."

Sammy pulled out her business card and a pen from her purse. "I'll write my cellphone number on the back of my card. Will you call me as soon as you find out anything?"

"I will." Jane popped out of her chair and shook Sammy's hand. "Thanks for coming in. I'll be in touch as soon as I find out anything."

Sammy turned and walked out into the

sunshine. One step closer to her goal. One step closer to making amends.

If Jane could find out who owns the trust and *if* the owner would consider selling the place.

CHAPTER 5

Sammy was at loose ends after her trip to the real estate office. She thought about going back out to Lighthouse Point, but decided to poke around town and see what had changed in the years since she left. She wandered through the general store—appropriately named The General Store. It was still a mix of souvenirs, hardware, and a few groceries in the back. She browsed through the t-shirts wondering if she should buy another one. She found a pale pink shirt with the lighthouse and "make a wish" imprinted on it. She bought it and walked back out into the sunshine.

She decided to treat herself to something at The Sweet Shoppe. A piece of pie or some bakery treat sounded good. She pushed through the door and the amazing aroma of yeast and cinnamon swirled around her. A woman with striking green eyes smiled and greeted her.

"Hi, welcome to The Sweet Shoppe. Didn't I see you here yesterday?" The woman led her to a table by the window.

"You did. I decided to come back and try a pastry. I was told you have the best in town."

"Ah, and who told you that?" The woman smiled. "I'm Julie, by the way. This is my restaurant."

"Nice to meet you, Julie. I'm Sammy. Harry Moorehouse told me to come back and try your pastries."

"Good old Harry. He's got quite a fondness for my almond scones."

"Then I'll try one. And a cup of coffee, please."

Julie left then came back with the pastry and a mug of coffee. She set them on the table. "So, how do you know Harry?"

"We were… friends… many years ago. Ran into him when I came back to town."

"He's a good guy."

"Yes, he is."

"Well, let me know if you'd like anything else."

"I will, thanks." Sammy took a bite of the almond scone and reveled in the delicate flavors.

Harry was right, the pastry *was* delicious. If she kept eating like this she was going to really put on the pounds this trip.

She watched people walk by out the window while she sat and sipped her coffee. Families headed to the beach on this unusually warm winter day. Couples walking arm in arm.

Loneliness descended over her, which was silly. She was used to being alone. She'd developed being alone to a fine art. But back here on Belle Island where she used to spend so much time with her family—back when it used to be an actual family—and where she spent so much time hanging out with Harry, well, the town just floated around her now without her feeling like she was a part of it. She shook her head. She was being silly. But in spite of insisting she was foolish, she paid her bill and went off to Island Property Management to see if she could track down Harry.

She hurried down the street and entered Island Property Management. Maybe they would know where Harry was working today, out repairing or working on one of their properties.

The perky receptionist greeted her. "Ah, Miss Thompson. Is there a problem with your rental?"

"No, no problem. I was just wondering... well, do you know where Harry Moorehouse is?"

The woman nodded. "Of course. He's in his office."

"He has an office here?"

"Yes…" The woman looked at her strangely. "Hey, Harry. Someone to see you." The woman called out.

Harry came out of a doorway off to the side and stopped short when he saw her. "Sammy."

"Hi, Harry. I just thought…" What had she thought? That he could come play with her like when they were kids?

"Come in." He motioned to his office and she crossed over and followed him into the room.

Light from the open window danced across his wooden desk. The desk was covered in neat stacks of papers. She glanced over at some plaques on the wall. Business of the Year. Community Youth Center Sponsor. A simple wooden nameplate rested on the desk. Harry Moorehouse - Owner.

"Harry, you *own* Island Property Management?"

It stung a bit the way Sammy asked the question, like she was surprised he could possibly own the business. Though, to be honest, he was still surprised a bit himself.

"Yes, it's mine. I kind of fell into it. Started managing a few properties and the business just grew."

"When you came to my cottage, I thought you were a repair guy for the company. You let me think that."

"I... did. I don't know why. I just, well you assumed that was all I'd ever made of myself and I didn't want to brag about all of this."

"Harry, I always thought you'd do great things. I'm not surprised you own the company. You're smart and a hard worker."

Harry smiled self-consciously. "Thanks."

Silence fell between them. He shifted from foot to foot. Sammy let her purse and the package she'd been carrying slip to the chair in front of the desk.

He cleared his throat. "So, you were looking for me?"

"I... I was. I am." A sheepish look flashed across Sammy's face. "I was just feeling out of place here on Belle Island and you're the only one that makes me feel... grounded... here."

"I do?" He cocked his head.

"You do. You're familiar and comfortable and..."

"Is that supposed to be a compliment?"

A rosy blush spread across Sammy's face. "Yes, it

is. I wanted to know if… if you'd like to come over to dinner tonight. I know we said we'd go out on an official date but didn't make definite plans. I thought I could cook dinner for you?"

Harry paused, not liking the unsettling feeling coursing through him. "Tonight?"

"If you already have plans, I understand. It's really last minute." Sammy took a step back.

"No, I don't have plans. I'd like that."

"So six-ish?

"Six it is. Can I bring anything?"

"No, I've got it."

Sammy picked up her purse and package and started for the door.

"Hey, Sammy?"

She paused and turned back towards him. "Yes?"

"Thanks for the invite." He flashed a grin at her. "And this *will* be called an official date."

She smiled and disappeared out the door.

This was three days in a row he'd seen Sammy Thompson again. He either really liked that fact or it scared him to death.

Sammy wasn't sure why she'd invited Harry over for

dinner. She wasn't the world's best cook, not even close. She did make a mean pasta carbonara though. She'd picked up the ingredients to make that and a tossed salad. She'd also grabbed some ice cream and chocolate sauce to make sundaes for dessert. Then she grabbed beer and some wine, not knowing which Harry would prefer. Probably the beer though. Nothing fancy, but it would have to do.

She set the table with placemats she found in a drawer and then searched the internet for fancy ways to fold the napkins. She'd no idea why she was going to so much trouble. After carefully setting a napkin folded to look like a flower on each plate, she tackled the meal prep.

She simmered the sauce for the pasta, and the cottage filled with the zesty aroma. She made up the salad and put it in the fridge. Promptly at six she looked up when she heard Harry knock on the French doors off the deck. She took a quick look around and motioned for him to come in.

"Here, these are for you." Harry held out a bouquet of fresh flowers.

He stood with the light filtering around him and she swore he looked like a Greek god or a male model or a TV star. She looked down at her bare feet, jeans, and t-shirt and self-consciously tucked wisps of her hair behind her ear.

Take the flowers. Her hands reached out to where Harry stood awkwardly holding out the bouquet.

"Oh, thank you. They're so pretty. I love flowers."

"I remember." Harry tossed her an uncomfortable smile.

Of course he remembered. Harry always remembered the little details.

She rooted around in the cabinets, found an old mason jar, and placed the flowers in it. She turned to Harry. "So I have beer or red wine. Got a preference?"

"Beer."

"Thought so." She pulled a bottle of beer from the fridge and handed it to Harry.

He twisted off the top and took a swig. "Ah. That's good."

She poured herself a glass of wine. "I thought we could sit outside for a bit before dinner?"

"Sounds good to me. Busy day. I could use some time to unwind."

They settled into chairs on the deck while the light sea breeze drifted across the sand and lifted the tendrils of hair surrounding her flushed face.

"So what all did you do today? Go into Sarasota

to see your client?" Harry stretched out his long, tanned legs, at ease with the relaxing seaside.

"No, the appointment got postponed until tomorrow. I just... I just wandered around town a bit." She didn't know why she didn't tell him about peeking into her grandparents' cottage or meeting with the real estate agent. Maybe because she wasn't ready to explain why she so desperately wanted to buy the cottage now that she'd concocted her plan. He wouldn't understand without knowing the whole story about that night so long ago, and she wasn't ready to tell anyone about the horrible thing she'd done. How she'd destroyed her family with her recklessness.

Harry watched as Sammy's delicate fingers wrapped around her wine glass. She took a small sip as she gazed at the ocean. He could sit and stare at her all night, comparing the adult Sammy to the young Sammy he'd known. The younger Sammy had been all bravado and confidence. This version was a bit more reserved. She paused a lot when she talked, as if she were choosing just the right words instead of blurting out her thoughts like she had when she was younger, a trait he'd found endearing if sometimes maddening.

Sammy turned to look at him and smiled. That smile. The one he remembered so well. He desperately searched for a subject. Any subject. "So do you like working with your father?"

"I do. He's taught me a lot. I got my MBA from Northwestern, but I've learned the most on the job. He wants me to take over the company when he retires, but that's a long way off and I have a lot to learn."

"Wow, you have everything all planned out."

"You seem to have your life planned out, too."

"I honestly just fell into this job. I like it. Like being my own boss. I think I'm good at it. But there wasn't much planning involved. It just happened."

"Where do you live now?" Sammy brought her wine glass up to her lips, not that he was staring again.

"I have an apartment over Island Property Management, but I spend a lot of time living in different cottages and condos that I renovate for the owners."

"You always were so handy and could fix anything." Sammy rose. "I'm going to finish up dinner. You just sit here and rest and I'll call you when it's ready."

"I could help."

"I've got it." Sammy disappeared inside.

Harry sat, drank his beer, and watched the waves march up the shore. This week had thrown him for a loop. He hadn't imagined seeing Sammy ever again, and yet here she was.

He amicably came inside when called and they sat at the table. Their conversation wavered between awkward silence and comfortable chitchat about their lives now. He couldn't keep himself from watching her every move. The graceful way she picked up her glass, her quick smile when he regaled her with stories of the island, the self-conscious way she kept tucking wisps of her hair behind her ears.

He stood after dinner, helped her with the dishes, then they went back out to the deck. "Want to sit on the swing?" He didn't ask her just so she'd sit next to him. He didn't.

They sat on the swing and he slowly pushed it with his foot, enjoying the gentle sway and ignoring that Sammy was just inches away from him. Their arms brushed and goosebumps crawled up his side. She smiled up at him. That smile. Again.

It was his undoing.

He leaned down and slowly pressed a kiss against her lips. A small gasp escaped her, then she kissed him back. One of her hands reached up and touched his face. He pressed his palm over her hand. Her hand that branded his cheek and made him hers. Hers again after all these years.

She pulled away slightly, looking directly into his eyes. "I'm not sure we should have done that." Sammy stood abruptly. "I should go in. Have an early day tomorrow."

Harry leveraged off the swing, his heart hammering and his thoughts swirling. "You okay?"

Sammy cleared her throat "Of course. I'm fine. I just… I should go in."

She turned to go and he caught her hand. "I'm sure we *should* have done that. I still feel it, Sams. The feeling. It's still there. I know you felt it, too."

"I… I'm not sure about this…"

He reached out and brushed his knuckles gently across her cheek. "It doesn't have to be confusing." He brought his hand back to his side. "I'll see you tomorrow?"

Sammy nodded and slipped inside. He headed down the stairs to the beach and walked to the water's edge, hoping the sea would cool his jangled nerves. The problem was, he was afraid that if he returned to Sea Haven tomorrow Sammy might be gone without a word, just like last time.

CHAPTER 6

Tally waved to her friends as they entered Magic Cafe after the lunch crowd had thinned. Susan and Julie waved back as Tally motioned them to a table by the edge of the sand. She grabbed a pitcher of tea and headed over to join them.

Julie gave her a quick hug before she sat down. "I was glad I could get away. I've been busy. Who knew that this time of year would bring so many weddings to the island? I swear I'm seeing wedding cakes in my sleep."

"I know. The inn has three weddings this month, not that I'm complaining." Susan reached for the pitcher and poured three tall glasses of sweet tea. "Jamie and I have been working crazy hours to keep up, but he insisted I take a break this afternoon. I'm not complaining, though. It's been great to fill the inn, week after week."

"How's married life treating you?" Tally slipped into a chair beside her friends.

Susan set down her glass. "I'm happier than one person has the right to be. It's been an adjustment, though, with Adam and his mother moving into the cottage with me. Jamie and Cindy temporarily moved to a small rental Harry found for them. We've been talking about building another cottage on the property for them to live in."

"That sounds like a fabulous idea. Everyone will get their space, but Jamie will still be on the inn's property." Tally nodded in agreement with the plan, not that they needed her approval, but she was glad to see things working out for her friend.

"How's Adam's mom doing?" Julie took a sip of her tea.

Julie was wearing one of her inevitable t-shirts with a saying on it. The woman did love her t-shirts. This one proclaimed "Today's good mood is brought to you by coffee. Lots of coffee."

Susan shrugged her shoulders. "She's doing fine enough. I know he worries about her Alzheimer's progressing, but for now things are going well. Adam was anxious about her adjusting to the move, but she seems to love working at the inn part time, and she and Dorothy have hit it off and spend time at the knitting group."

Dorothy had worked at the inn for as long as Tally could remember, back when Susan's brother had owned the inn. Tally had some long-time employees at Magic Cafe, but none who had been with her as long as Dorothy had been with the inn. "I'm glad it's working out for all of you."

Tally turned to Julie. "So what about you? How are the wedding plans coming?"

"Well, I have my wedding cake planned, does that count?"

"Of course you do. I'd expect no less from a baker like you." Susan laughed. "But what can we help you with?"

"You're doing enough just letting us have the wedding at the inn."

"Have you looked at dresses? Thought about flowers? Invitations?"

"All I know is I want it to be a small service and simple."

"Adam's and my wedding was simple and I loved it."

"Great, can we just duplicate what you did?" Julie grinned.

"Don't you worry, we'll help you with everything." Tally waved for Tereza.

The waitress came over and Tally introduced her to her friends. "Tereza, this is Susan—she owns Belle Island Inn, and this is Julie—she owns The Sweet Shoppe."

"Nice to meet you." Tereza smiled at the women.

"Tereza is new to the area. A great worker. I'm glad to have her. The customers love her." Tally extolled the virtues of her new hire. She really like the girl and she was very reliable, which counted for a lot in Tally's book.

"Glad to have you here, Tereza. That's high praise from Tally." Susan smiled at the waitress.

"Well, I love my job here and I love the area. Much nicer than the winter in the Midwest where I came from." Tereza took out her pad. "Can I take your orders?"

The women ordered then Tally poured them all more tea. "So, I have news."

"What's that?" Julie raised an eyebrow.

"Harry came to dinner here the other night. You know who was with him? Sammy Thompson."

"Do I know her?" Julie's forehead wrinkled.

"She used to come to the island when she was young. Stayed with her grandparents, though they don't live here anymore. I think she stopped coming to the island about the time you arrived here. I always thought Harry and Sammy had a thing going back then. At least Harry was smitten by her. By the looks of things, I think he still is."

"Jamie said something about it, too. He went to lunch with Harry yesterday." Susan shook her head. "He said Harry was a goner. That Sammy was, is, and always will be his Achilles' heel. I guess she left without a word all those years ago and Jamie is a bit worried now. Harry's such a nice man, I hope he doesn't get hurt. I'd love for him to find someone to settle down with though."

"I'm not sure Harry will ever settle down. Not after what happened to Rose. We all know it's not his fault, but I don't think he'll ever forgive himself." Julie sighed.

"Well, he does deserve to move on and be happy. He's a good man. I guess we'll just have to see what happens." Tally leaned back in her chair and their talk turned to the weather.

The three friends ate their late lunch, then Susan headed back to the inn and Julie to The Sweet Shoppe. Tally cleared the table and slowly walked to her small office. Tereza poked her head in and said she was going to do a double shift because one of the other waitresses had gone home sick. Tally thanked her lucky stars for finding Tereza.

Tally sat at her desk and mindlessly shifted through the stacks of papers. Her thoughts were on Julie. She could tell that Julie was overwhelmed with the whole wedding thing. She wasn't convinced her friend believed she deserved the happiness she'd found with Reed, and Tally didn't know how to fix that. And not being able to fix a problem her friend had bothered Tally. She was a fixer. A mender of fences. But she was afraid this would only be put right with time and Reed's love for Julie.

Sammy pulled over the bridge to Belle Island late afternoon. She didn't think her presentation at Adriana Boutiques went well today. She'd been distracted, and her thoughts kept wandering back to Harry. Her father was going to be so disappointed if she messed up this deal. It was the first big deal he'd allowed her to do alone. She'd promised him she could handle it. Now what if she let him down?

She didn't feel like being alone at the cottage, so she pulled into a parking spot on Oak Avenue. She climbed out of the car and looked left and right. A bright sign caught her eye. The Lucky Duck.

Great, she could use some luck. She walked down the sidewalk and entered the building. As her eyes adjusted to the dimness, she saw a long counter along one wall. She slipped onto a barstool.

The man behind the bar slid a bowl of pretzels and nuts her way and smiled. "Be with you in a sec."

The man returned with a friendly smile and a menu. "Eating? Drinking? What can I get for you?"

"I'll have a beer for now." She glanced at the long list of beers on the back of the menu and picked one.

He came back with a frosty mug and a bottle of beer and placed it in front of her. "I'm Willy. Let me know if I can get you anything else."

"Thanks, Willy." She took a small sip of the icy drink. She pulled a notebook from her purse and started jotting notes on a new strategy for her approach with her client.

Willy came back to check on her. "Anything else?"

"Not right now."

He nodded at her notebook. "In town for business?"

"I work for an ad agency. Trying to land a client

in Sarasota, but not having the luck I'd hoped I would."

Willy looked up and waved to a red-haired man walking into the bar. "Hey, Jamie. Over here."

The man walked over.

"This here is… what's your name?" Willie raised an eyebrow.

"Sammy Thompson." The red-haired man answered for her. She turned and looked at him closely. "Jamie?"

"In the flesh. Long time."

"It has been. You look… the same, yet different."

"Harry said you were in town."

"So you two know each other?" Willie stood looking at both of them.

"When we were young. We both came here to the island in the summers."

"Well, Sammy here is an advertiser person. Didn't you say that Adam was looking for someone to handle an advertising campaign for Hamilton Hotels?"

"I did. He is." Jamie leaned his head to one side as if deciding if she were up for the challenge. "Want me to hook you up with Adam? He just married my mom. He's working on managing the re-opening of

The Hamilton in Sarasota and then The Beverly in Tampa. He's wanting a PR campaign to rebrand the hotels. I could set you up with a meeting with him."

"You can? That would be great. I'd love to talk to him and see what he needs."

Jamie pulled out his phone and wrote on the back of a coaster. "Here's his cell phone number. I'll talk to him tonight and let him know you're going to call."

"I really appreciate this."

"Hope you can help him out." Jamie turned to Willie. "Got those sandwiches for me?"

"Yep, let me go grab them."

Jamie turned back to Sammy. "Harry said you two went out the other night."

"We did and he came over last night and I cooked for him."

Jamie's forehead wrinkled. "I know Harry was happy to see you again, but Sammy..."

"What?" Sammy eyed Jamie.

"Try not to up and disappear on him without a word this time."

Well, one thing was sure. No one in this small town ever forgot anything. Sammy nodded. "I won't. We're just friends, though."

A friend who kissed her. A friend who occupied

her every thought today. A friend whose kiss she couldn't get out her mind.

~

Harry shuffled the papers on his desk, not really seeing them, not getting anything accomplished. Well, except for thinking about Sammy. He'd thought about her all day long. He needed to talk to her. See how she was. He shouldn't have kissed her, though honestly nothing could have prevented him from wanting that kiss last night.

She'd kissed him back. She had. Even with her protests that it had been a mistake.

It was no mistake.

Maybe it was even fate.

Maybe he'd been given another chance with her.

Maybe he was a clueless fool…

He was getting ahead of himself. It's just that seeing her again brought back all those hidden feelings. But they were different people now. They couldn't just take up where they left off, could they?

He wished he could tell her what he was doing with her grandparents' cottage, too. Well, it wasn't Sammy's grandparents' cottage anymore. They'd sold it years ago. Anyway, he couldn't tell her. Not yet. He had to tell someone else first.

He was on a short deadline and needed to get the cottage finished. Not that it would ever make right what had happened, what he'd caused, but maybe it would ease his guilt. The guilt that ate at him the last ten years. Now he had a chance to change things, to make things up to Rose, to make her life easier. Not that he deserved happiness after what he'd done. Rose had never blamed him, but he blamed himself. It had all been such a pointless, stupid dare. One he wished he could take back. But he couldn't.

Rose was always in his thoughts.

Rose, the woman he'd put into a wheelchair.

CHAPTER 7

Harry walked down the beach to Sweet Haven. Scattered stars lit the evening sky and a strong breeze rushed in from the sea. He wondered how Sammy's day went in Sarasota, that's all it was. He was sticking with that as his excuse to see her. It wasn't that he couldn't stand for her to be a handful of doors down the beach and *not* see her. It wasn't that. It wasn't.

Okay, *maybe* it was nothing but an excuse to see her. A small part of him was afraid that he'd get to the cottage and Sammy would be gone, vanished in the night like before.

Okay, *maybe* it wasn't a small part of him that thought that. It was more like every fiber of his being was afraid she'd be gone.

The lights were on inside, and his pulse raced at the sight. Then he saw her sitting on the deck. He stopped and looked at her, with her hair flying in the breeze, lost in thought.

As if she could feel his gaze, she turned towards him. She waved her hand and he started up the beach toward her.

The wooden stairs were dusted with a layer of sand as he climbed up to the deck. "Hey, Sams."

"Hey." Sammy sat curled up in an Adirondack chair with a light wrap draped around her shoulders. A pink wrap, of course.

"Just thought I'd drop by and see how you're doing."

"I'm fine. Have a seat." She motioned to the chair beside her.

He dropped to the seat and stretched out his legs. He sucked in a deep breath. "So are you mad at me for stealing that kiss last night?" He figured he'd just jump right into the deep end.

"I'm pretty sure you didn't steal it. I'm certain I kissed you back."

He grinned. "I'm sure you did, too."

"I was just… surprised. That's all."

"Hey, I kind of surprised myself."

"Harry?"

"Hm?"

"The kiss was nice." Sammy smiled that make-his-world-spin-out-of-control smile.

"Glad to hear it." He was probably grinning like a teenager with a crush and didn't even care. "Maybe we could do it again."

"I bet we could."

He leaned over and kissed her gently on her lips. She kissed him back with no hesitation. He reluctantly pulled away. He couldn't just sit there and kiss her all night, could he?

Hm… *maybe?*

Sammy reached over and her small fingers wrapped around his hand, connecting them, making all the years they were apart crumble away.

Sammy sat in silence, content to just hold Harry's strong hand. The stars danced above them like Christmas lights blowing in the breeze. Harry lifted their hands and kissed her fingers. A shiver raced through her.

"You cold?"

"A bit." She pulled her hand from his and tugged the wrap tighter around her shoulders.

Harry reached out his hand. "Here."

She put her hand in his and he pulled her onto

his lap. She snuggled closer, allowing his warmth to spread through her. It wasn't really that chilly tonight, but all of her senses were raw and jittery. He ran a hand up and down her arm and she tucked her head against him. He kissed the top of her head and they sat together while she lost herself in memories.

"So, did you have a good day?" His rumbly voice pulled her from her thoughts.

"I did." She tried to concentrate on something other than his arm wrapped around her shoulder and his deep, steady breathing. "Well, at first things weren't going so well. I'm not sure I landed the account in Sarasota. I'll try again tomorrow when I actually meet with Adriana."

"Sorry it didn't go well." Harry's hand continued to travel up and down her arm.

"But I ran into Jamie at The Lucky Duck."

"You did?" Harry's hand stopped.

"He gave me Adam's phone number—the guy who married his mom. The Hamilton Hotel company is looking for a new ad agency for a promotion for their two new hotels down here. I'm supposed to call him tomorrow to set up a meeting to talk about what they need. If I could land that account, maybe Father won't be so disappointed if I don't get the Adriana Boutiques account."

"Well, I hope it goes well for you. So maybe you'll be staying longer?"

"I'm not sure yet. If nothing goes right, I might be done with all the ad agency business tomorrow." She could see the disappointment in Harry's eyes. "But, there's something else I'm planning to do while I'm down here. Something I need to do to try and make things right."

"What's that?" He ran a finger along her lips, making it hard to concentrate.

"I... I'm trying to buy back my grandparents' cottage."

Harry sucked in a harsh breath. He stood up, taking her with him, set her firmly on her feet, and took a step back. He looked right into her eyes, a hard look on his face. "You can't."

CHAPTER 8

Sammy looked up at Harry. "Why not? I'm going to try. The cottage isn't officially for sale, but I have a real estate agent looking into contacting the owners. It's held in a trust and she's trying to find out who to contact to make an offer."

Harry's face hardened into a determined scowl. "There's no way that cottage is going to be sold."

"Why not? I *need* to buy it. I want to give it to my grandparents. It will… well, I hope it will start to heal my family and make amends for what I did." Her eyes flashed with a determination of their own.

"What did you do that you need to make amends for?"

"You know that day? The day I left the island for good?" She tilted her face up to look at him.

"How could I forget that? I know we haven't talked about your mother or what happened—"

"Or the fact I just disappeared and I couldn't face coming back. Everything fell apart that night. It was the beginning of the end for my family."

"I know it was. I wish I could have taken it back. Made it all go away."

"But it *did* happen and nothing has ever been the same."

"I'm so sorry, Sammy."

"Well, it wasn't your fault."

"I'm still sorry it happened."

"You know, I still feel like it was all my fault. If we hadn't gone to Blue Heron Island, none of this would have happened. I reacted so badly, too."

"I'm not sure there is a good way to react to what we saw." After all these years she was blaming herself? Astonishment washed over him. How could she think any of that was her fault? Their timing had been lousy but it sure wasn't *her* fault.

"I wish we hadn't gone there. Hadn't seen…"

"It was your *mother's* failing, not yours. She was the one cheating on your father. She was the one we saw kissing John Eatherton. How can any of that be *your* fault?"

"Our family fell apart that night. If I wouldn't have gone to the island with you… I know you

were hoping that I would sleep with you that day…
and I planned to. I was ready to. But if I hadn't
picked that day to sleep with you…"

"And yet, we never did, did we?" Harry
remembered every agonizing minute of that
afternoon. All the preparations he'd made to make
the day perfect for Sammy. The boat ride to the
island and how nervous he'd been. The picnic
lunch he'd made for them. A portable tape player
with a mix of Sammy's favorite romantic songs.
He'd even planned to tell her that he loved her…
because he had. She'd been his whole world
back then.

But they'd been at the wrong place at the
wrong time.

They'd taken the path to a deserted part of Blue
Heron Island then stopped when they'd heard
voices. He'd been so disappointed, scrambling to
think of another area of the island they could go to.

But then everything changed. Sammy had taken
one look, her eyes wide in disbelief and collapsed
against him in silence, grabbing onto his arm,
frozen. There was Sammy's mother laughing and
kissing another man. A man who wasn't her father.
He'd pulled her back into the darkness of the
pathway and held her steady.

He remembered the moment clearly. It was the

first time his heart had broken for someone else's pain.

Her mother and John had sprinted across the beach, oblivious that they'd been spotted, and lunged into the sea, laughing and dunking each other in the waves.

Then Sammy turned deathly white, pushed away, and raced back to the boat. He'd left everything there on the path and raced after her. They hadn't said a word on the ride back to Belle Island. She'd climbed out of the boat, given him a sad look, and turned and walked away. That was the last memory he had of her, and it had haunted him for years.

"I came by the next morning to make sure you were okay, but your grandmother said you'd gone. I never knew why you left without talking to me. You never answered any of my letters."

"I know, I'm sorry. I made *so* many mistakes that day…"

Sammy stood and turned to him, a haunted look on her face. "I can't talk about this anymore. Maybe I shouldn't have come back to the island." She swept her hair away from her face and let out a long breath.

"It's getting late. I better go inside."

"But I still need to talk to you." Harry reached out and touched her arm.

"Not tonight, Harry." With that, she slipped into the cottage.

He didn't think any of this was Sammy's fault... but he understood her feeling that way. He had a heck of a load of guilt that he carried around himself.

He didn't even get a chance to tell her why there was no way she could buy back her grandparents' cottage.

CHAPTER 9

S usan looked up when Adam entered her office at Belle Island Inn. She smiled at him. She still couldn't believe she was married to him, this happy, and the inn was out of financial danger. "Hi, sweetheart. Headed to Sarasota?"

"I am." He crossed the distance, leaned over, and kissed her.

There was something so comforting and reassuring about being kissed goodbye each day and kissed hello when he returned home. She reached up and touched his face, and he smiled.

"I'll be back by dinner, I hope. Oh, and I just talked to that woman, Samantha, about an advertising campaign for Hamilton Hotels. She's going to put something together for me. She had some good ideas off the top of her head. Very creative person."

"Well, I hope it works out for both of you. She's a friend of Harry's. Maybe more than a friend."

"That's what Jamie said. Anyway, I was impressed with her. We'll have to see what she comes up with."

They both looked up to see Adam's mother, Mary, standing in the doorway.

"Hi, Mary. You need something?" Susan smiled at the woman she'd come to care so much for in the last months.

"I was just looking for…" Mary's forehead wrinkled. "My… oh, what do you call it?"

Adam crossed to the doorway. "I'll help you. What did you lose?"

"You know that floral thing."

"Your knitting bag?"

"Yes, that's it. My knitting bag. Don't know why I couldn't think of the word for it."

Adam flashed a worried look toward Susan. She could feel his concern. It wasn't easy watching his mother struggle for words and get confused.

Susan stood. "You go ahead and go into work. I'll help Mary find her knitting."

"Thank you, dear. I'm in the middle of knitting a baby…" Mary's eyes clouded.

"A baby afghan. You showed it to me last night. We'll find it."

Adam kissed her again quickly and mouthed "thank you" and left. Susan took Mary's arm and they went off to hunt for the missing bag.

Sammy sat at the table at Sweet Haven with her notebook in front of her. She swore she got better ideas when she scribbled them on paper than when she tried to brainstorm and type them into her laptop. She needed to fine-tune some ideas to present to Adam for the Hamilton Hotel promotion as well as work on a new angle for her other account. *If* it became her account.

Her phone rang and she snatched it off the table.

"Samantha?"

"Yes?"

"This is Jane Munson."

"Hi, Jane." Sammy set her pen on the table. "What did you find out?"

"Well, I did look into the trust that holds the title for the deed for the cottage you're interested in, and I was able to find out the name of the trustee."

Sammy's pulse quickened. "That's great."

"I have a call in to him."

"Wonderful." Sammy knew it was a long shot that he'd want to sell, but she was prepared to make a generous offer.

"His name is Harry Moorehouse, the owner of Island Property Management here in town."

Sammy's heart plummeted, followed quickly by a wave of anger. Harry had said nothing last night when she'd told him she wanted to buy the cottage. Oh, he'd said she couldn't buy it, but not *why* she couldn't.

Because *he* was the trustee for the trust that held the deed to the cottage.

"Thank you for letting me know." Sammy clicked off the phone and stood. She didn't know what Harry was up to, or why he didn't tell her he controlled the cottage, but she was going to find out.

She was going to find out *right now*.

Harry looked up as Sammy slammed through the doorway to his office, her eyes blazing.

"So, when were you going to tell me that *you* are the trustee on my grandparents' cottage?"

Harry stood. "I was trying to tell you last night.

You cut me off. I was going to come over after work tonight and try again."

"So, that's why you said I can't buy it? Because you own it?" Her cheeks flushed red with anger.

"I don't technically *own* it. I'm the trustee for the *trust* that owns it."

"Same thing."

"Not the same thing at all."

"Well, I want to make an offer on the cottage."

"The cottage isn't available for sale. It's just not possible." Harry reached out to touch Sammy, but she jerked away.

"Because you won't sell it to me? I *told* you I want to get it back for my grandparents. It's important. It's imperative. It's... I *need* to buy it."

"Sammy, you aren't listening. I *can't* sell it. It's just not possible."

Sammy lifted her chin in defiance. "Why not?"

Harry drug in a long, slow breath. "Well, I'm not at liberty to say. At least not yet."

"You know I want the cottage—*need* the cottage—yet you won't sell it... and you won't tell me why? Why is it so important that you have *my* family's cottage?" Sammy lifted her face to look directly into his eyes.

"Be honest, Sams. It's not your family's cottage. It hasn't been in over eighteen years."

"You know what I mean." Her brown eyes crackled with anger.

"I would explain it all if I could. But I've made promises. I just can't break them. I'm sorry. I'd tell you everything if I could."

"Right." There was no missing the sarcasm in her voice.

He reached out again and touched her arm. She reached down slowly and plucked his hand away.

"I told you it was important to me, to my family. That I needed to set things right. If I can't buy it back... I can't make things right. But you don't care."

"I *do* care. But buying back the cottage is just... impossible."

"We'll see about that." Sammy whirled around and slammed back out of his office.

He slunk into his chair and put his head in his hands. He was between the proverbial rock and a hard place. There were two women he deeply cared for and both needed the same cottage.

Sammy stalked into Sweet Haven and tossed her purse on a chair. She opened cabinets and banged them closed, trying to remember which of the stupid cabinets held the glasses. She found them on the third attempt, yanked opened the fridge, and pulled out a bottle of sparkling water. She filled the glass and took a long drink, then slammed the glass on the counter. She didn't know why Harry was being so difficult, and at this point she didn't care. She'd told him how important it was to her to get the cottage back.

Though, she hadn't told him the whole reason. How it was *her fault* that her grandparents lost the cottage in the first place. Despair slipped over her. She couldn't fail now. Not after she'd found the perfect solution to help atone for her mistakes.

Her phone rang and she snatched it off the counter.

"It's Jane Munson again." Jane's perky voice came through the phone.

"I know, Harry said no." Sammy tried to control the angry tone in her voice.

"What? Well, yes he did. But a friend of mine at the recorder's office said there has been some recent inquiries into the deed on the cottage. She's actually waiting for some legal documents to be sent to her."

"I don't understand." Sammy impatiently swept her hair away from her face.

"There might be some questions on the status of

the deed to the property. I should know more in a few days."

"So the trust might not legally own the cottage?"

"I'm not sure, but it seems like someone thinks they still have a legal claim to the property."

"You'll let me know as soon as you find out something?"

"I will."

Sammy set the phone on the counter and took another sip of the cold water. All was not lost. She might *still* find a way to get the cottage back for her grandparents.

CHAPTER 10

Sammy went to the Sweet Shoppe the next morning for breakfast. She kept thinking she'd go get groceries if her stay kept getting extended, but so far she'd just made sure she had coffee and the items she'd picked up to make dinner for Harry. Not that that would happen again. She didn't care if she ever saw him again. She didn't know why he was so set against her getting her grandparents' cottage back again, but now she at least had a glimmer of hope from what her real estate agent had said.

She sat at a table, ordered coffee and a cinnamon roll, and bided her time watching the customers come and go. She had an hour to kill before she needed to head out to Sarasota for her meeting with Hamilton Hotels.

Tally came in and spoke with Julie for a moment, then headed over to greet Sammy. "Hey, there. Mind if I join you? I came to pick up Julie, but she's not quite ready to go."

"Please, sit down. I'd love the company."

A waitress brought over coffee as Tally slid into the chair across the table.

"Are you having a good stay on the island?" Tally took a sip of her steaming coffee.

"I am. It's a bit strange being back here after all this time though."

"I bet. Twenty years is a long time."

"So many things are the same, and yet, so much has changed."

"I see you and Harry are still friends. Or back to being friends." Tally smiled.

"Well, we were... but, I'm not sure now. I think we've just changed so much. Harry is different now. More secretive. Just... different."

"He is different than the boy he used to be. He's had a few... *complications* in his life."

Sammy looked closely at Tally. "What kind of complications?"

Tally paused and looked thoughtful. "I guess I'm not talking out of school here, because it's common knowledge." She leaned back in her chair. "Harry had a good friend here after you left. Rose.

She moved to the island about fifteen years ago. Never was quite sure if they were dating or just good friends. Harry took Rose to a waterpark one weekend. I guess he dared her to climb up for a trip down a really tall water slide that she didn't really want to go on. But she did, because Harry dared her. The slide collapsed and Rose was hurt. I don't think Harry ever forgave himself, not that it's really his fault."

"I didn't know…"

"He changed a lot after that. Worked hard at his business. Settled down. The endearing bit of boyish charm and joy he'd always had left him."

"He didn't say anything about this to me."

"Not something he really talks about. He's still been a great friend to Rose though. The town held a fund raiser he coordinated to help pay Rose's way to college after she spent years in rehab. She never regained the use of her legs, though."

"Wow, that's just really rough, isn't it? I can see why he feels guilty. It's strange how just a few words we say can change so many things, isn't it?"

"I never really thought of it that way, but you're right. Decisions we make sometimes have far-reaching consequences." Tally nodded slowly.

Sammy so understood the guilt that Harry felt. Maybe Harry would understand why she so badly needed to buy back the cottage if she would just tell him the whole story. Explain to him how she'd blown up her entire world and ruined her family. She'd go look for him tonight after she came back from Sarasota and try to explain.

Sammy straightened her skirt as she walked into the Hamilton Hotel. She'd scheduled a meeting with Adam Lyons and Cindy Hall—who she'd discovered was Jamie Hall's new wife. Cindy was working on redecorating the Hamilton Hotel and helping with the rebranding. Adam said Cindy knew so much about the hotel that he'd like her in on the meeting.

She crossed the lobby and told the receptionist that she was there to see Adam. Soon a man came striding across the lobby. "You must be Miss Thompson." He held out his hand.

She took his firm handshake and smiled. "Mr. Lyons?"

"Adam, please. Follow me. We'll go to our small conference room."

She followed him across the lobby wondering if she should have told him to call her Samantha. Why was she so nervous about this meeting? She was usually self-assured, at least in her business life. Her failure with the Adriana Boutiques account was shaking her confidence.

They entered a small, well-appointed conference room and a woman rose from her seat. "Hi, I'm Cindy."

"Nice to meet you Cindy. I really appreciate your husband, Jamie, giving my name to Adam."

"He was glad to help." Cindy sat down again.

Sammy set her leather tote on the table and pulled out her laptop. She connected it to the large TV screen at the end of the table. She drew in a deep breath. "Shall we get started? Now this is just preliminary thoughts and ideas. I wanted to get a better feel for what you were wanting, then I can do up a final presentation."

"That sounds great." Adam took a seat across from her. "We want to coordinate an advertising campaign highlighting the remodel of the Hamilton Hotel in Sarasota as well as The Beverly in Tampa. The Beverly has such a strong name recognition that we're intending to call it The Beverly Hamilton."

"That sounds like a smart choice. I'll show you some campaigns we've done and I'll need to get more information from you. I have some very tentative ideas I'll run past you just from the information you gave me when we spoke on the phone." She clicked on her computer and started her presentation.

The door to the conference room opened and a man poked his head inside. "I heard you all were in here."

Adam and Cindy rose. Adam crossed to the door and stretched out his hand. "Mr. Hamilton. I didn't expect you until later today."

"Got in early. Thought I'd pop in here and hear what Miss Thompson has to say. I was told her company is being considered for the advertising campaign." He crossed over and extended his hand to her. "Delbert Hamilton."

"Nice to meet you, Mr. Hamilton." Hamilton. As in *Hamilton* Hotels. Okay, this is not what she'd been expecting. She swallowed and pasted on what she hoped was a confident smile.

"Go on, continue. I'll just take a seat here." Mr. Hamilton sat down at the table.

Do not get nervous. You can do this.

Sammy continued, showcasing some ideas and asking questions about the image they wanted to project for these new hotels they'd added to the Hamilton Hotel chain. She took notes as they talked. It was clear that Mr. Hamilton wanted to make these two new hotels different than the standard Hamilton Hotel brand, set them apart, appeal to a less stuffy clientele. He wanted to have a more casual Florida lifestyle feel, while still showcasing excellent customer service and a luxurious setting.

After an hour of discussions, they all rose from the table. She hoped she could come up with a promotion that could hit exactly what they wanted.

As they walked back out to the lobby, a well-dressed woman approached them with two large shopping bags that she dropped at her feet. "Delbert, your driver just dropped me off from my shopping trip. I swear, it's getting harder and harder to find a good dress shop here."

From the looks of the full bags, it couldn't have been too hard, but Sammy kept her thoughts to herself.

"Camille, this is Miss Thompson. She's working up a promotion for our new hotels. Miss Thompson, this is Camille Montgomery." Mr. Hamilton eyed Camille's bags.

The woman looked her up and down then turned to Mr. Hamilton. "I tell you, your daddy isn't going to like what you've let Cindy do to this hotel. You'll probably let her ruin the Beverly in Tampa, too."

Cindy's face blushed a hot red.

"Camille, I've told you that I think Cindy's choices

have been spot on with the hotel. She has a good head for business and I appreciate hearing her input."

Camille ignored Mr. Hamilton's gentle admonition. "And this new ad agency? Where are they from? Not from here, I hope. You need to have experienced people working on your advertising."

"We're located in Chicago." Sammy wasn't sure whether she should enter into the conversation or not and wasn't sure what the size of a city had to do with the experience of a company.

"Ah, well. That's good. You look pretty young for an account this size though." Camille cocked her head to one side and a slight scowl crossed her perfectly made-up face.

"Camille, why don't we take your bags and get the driver to take you on over to Belle Island. I have more work to do. I'll get the driver to come back and pick me up later."

"You're always so busy now when we come down here." Camille's voice held the slightest whining edge to it.

"Camille, sweetheart, you know it's a lot of work to open these hotels. I'll take you out to eat tonight when I get to the island."

"Maybe I'll have Mama's chef fix us something. There's really no place nice to eat on the island."

Mr. Hamilton picked up the packages and followed as Camille swirled across the lobby.

Adam laughed after Camille was gone. "Good to know there's no place good to eat on the island. Like the restaurant at the inn or Magic Cafe."

Cindy turned to Sammy. "And that was Camille. She's been dating Mr. Hamilton for quite a while. She's not my biggest fan, as you can see." Cindy shrugged. "Anyway, it was good to meet you. Good luck coming up with a final presentation. You had some really creative ideas."

"It was nice meeting you, too."

Cindy walked away and Adam turned to her. "If you have any questions, feel free to call me. We'll talk again soon when you have your presentation ready."

"Yes, thank you for meeting with me."

Sammy walked out into the bright sunshine, slipping on her sunglasses against the glare. Near the entrance, Camille and Mr. Hamilton were having a rather strident conversation. She could catch snatches of their words.

"… running up bills again." Mr. Hamilton looked pointedly at Camille's packages.

She couldn't hear Camille's reply.

"Camille, darlin', I'm pretty sure you could look

in your closet and pick an outfit and never wear the same thing twice in three years' time."

Sammy heard every word of *that* comment. She smothered a smile, looked away, and headed to her car. She didn't want to get in Camille's line of fire, that's for sure.

~

Harry chastised himself all day for upsetting Sammy. Though, he didn't know what he could do differently. He wasn't at liberty to say why Sammy couldn't buy her grandparents' cottage back. Not yet. He wondered why they'd sold the cottage in the first place, if they wanted to come back now.

Maybe Sammy could look for another cottage for them? Though, it wouldn't be the same. But then, Bellemire wouldn't be the same now either. Not after all the work he'd done to it.

He looked up from his desk when he heard a noise at the door to his office. "Rose. I didn't know you were coming to town."

"Hey, Harry." Rose looked up with her always cheerful smile from her low position in her ever-present wheelchair. "Surprise. I'm in town."

He got up from his desk and crossed the room.

He leaned down to kiss Rose on the cheek. "It's a nice surprise though."

The woman rolled her wheelchair into his office and as always, the sight of the wheelchair tore at his heart and filled him with guilt.

"Harry, take that look off your face." Rose shook her head.

Rose hated it when he mentioned his guilt or she caught him staring at her with a remorseful expression. "Whatever you say." He abruptly slipped on a grin.

"That's better." Rose nodded approvingly. "You got plans tonight? Because I'm craving dinner at Magic Cafe."

"No, no plans." He'd intended to go and find Sammy and talk to her, try to smooth things over. But, if Rose wanted to go out to dinner, that was his priority. She was always his priority. "I'll come over about six?"

"Sounds great. I have something to show you when you get there."

"Another surprise?" He winked at her.

"Yep, I'm just full of surprises today." She turned and wheeled out of his office.

It was a week full of unexpected whammy after whammy for him, and his life kept tilting out of control.

CHAPTER 11

Harry arrived at Rose's small, first floor apartment promptly at six. The apartment was inland a bit, though Rose adored the ocean and he knew she'd love a view of it. But the apartment had been a convenient location to where she went to rehab, and all located on one floor. She'd been away at college except for summers and breaks for the last few years.

She was finally going to graduate this coming spring.

By then he'd have *his* surprise for her all ready.

Rose opened the door to his knock. "Ready for your surprise?" She grinned at him.

"I think so?" He looked at her skeptically.

"Okay, then. I'm driving."

"What?" Harry stepped back in surprise.

"See that red car over there?" Rose pointed to a four door sedan. "That's mine."

"But…"

"Harry, quit always thinking of me as the victim. The accident happened. We can't change that. Anyway… I learned to drive while I was away."

"But how?"

"Hand controls."

Harry broke into a full grin. "Of course you did. I wouldn't expect anything less from you. Come on. Take me for a spin."

Rose drove him all around the island, out to Lighthouse Point, then back to Magic Cafe. Even though it was a bit chilly, she rolled the windows down and the breeze tossed her blonde hair in the wind. She looked carefree and happy.

Maybe she was.

Maybe he could make her even happier.

Sammy headed to Magic Cafe for a quiet dinner. She still didn't feel motivated to get groceries and cook, so she figured another grouper sandwich, while she had the opportunity, was her best course of action.

Tally greeted her with a hug. "Good to see you. Couldn't keep away, could you?" The older woman flashed a smile full of warmth and welcome. Immediately Sammy's feelings of loneliness melted away.

"I couldn't stay away, you're right. It's just me tonight."

"Outside?"

"Yes, I brought my sweater." Sammy held up a warm sweater she'd grabbed. The January night air was chilly tonight, but Tally had turned on the heaters overhead and the patio glowed with a warm light.

Sammy paused when she saw Harry sitting at a table by the edge of the beach. A beautiful blonde woman sat beside him. Harry threw back his head and laughed out loud at some comment the woman made.

Then she saw the woman was sitting in a wheelchair.

So this was Rose.

The woman reached out and touched Harry's hand in an intimate gesture of familiarity.

Sammy's heart plummeted in a quick whoosh of loss and loneliness.

"Sammy, you coming?" Tally nodded toward the dining area.

"I… uh…"

Tally glanced over to where Sammy was looking. "Harry's here with Rose. You want to join them?"

"No… I…" Sammy eyes darted around, looking for an escape, then they were drawn back to the cozy scene at Harry and Rose's table.

Harry looked up right then and saw her staring at him. He jumped up from his chair and started weaving through the tables towards her.

Closer.

"You know, Tally. I don't think I'm very hungry after all."

Sammy turned and hurried out of Magic Cafe.

"Wait. Sammy." Harry's voice filtered through the dinner chatter going on at the cafe.

She didn't stop.

She couldn't.

She fled to the safety of her car and raced out of the parking lot, a spray of crushed shells flinging out from under her tires.

~

On the way home from Magic Cafe Harry asked Rose to stop at Bellemire Cottage.

"Why?"

"You'll see. I have something to show you."

"You fixing up this place for someone, too? You're really good at that, Harry."

She pulled into the drive. He got the wheelchair for her and she slipped into it. He pushed her through the front door and flipped on the lights. She slowly rolled further into the cottage, her face creased in a frown.

"I don't get it. It's all set up for... well for someone in a wheelchair. Lower light switches, wide doorways, and that bar over there has a lower counter."

"That's because the owner is in a wheelchair."

She turned to look at him. "Who's that?"

"You."

Her eyes widened. "What do you mean, me?"

"The cottage is yours. Well, when I finish fixing it up. Should have it ready by the time you graduate this spring."

"I can't afford it." She shook her head.

"It's already bought and paid for."

"By who?" Her eyes narrowed.

"Most of it is from the trust set up from the settlement from your accident. You know how you asked me to handle your funds. Well, let's just say I got really lucky on a few stocks I invested for you. Willie gave me some advice. Turns out he's pretty knowledgeable about investing. Then I bought this cottage for a song because the owners were divorcing and needed to get rid of it. It was a great investment for you, by the way, the market has rebounded and it's worth twice or more what I bought it for. I've been working on it for a long time. Slowly getting it ready for you."

"Harry, I can't accept it."

"Of course you can. You own it."

"But you did so much work on it. *Too much*. Harry, you do way too much for me. When will you ever forgive yourself? I don't blame you. You know that. It breaks my heart that you still blame yourself. It was a stupid accident. That's all it was."

"I thought you'd love the cottage and love living on the beach. You'll have a house with everything I could research that made living in a wheelchair easier. Wide doorways. Roll in shower. Those boxes over there are wheelchair height cabinets for the kitchen sink and stovetop. I have a lot of it wired for voice control. The thermostat, the blinds, the lights." He wanted her to love the place. To be happy.

"Harry, I do like this. I do." She grinned at him.

"And very cool that you invested my money so well for me. Who knows what other talents lurk behind your boyish good looks."

"Many talents, some more hidden than others." He smiled back at her. "So we're good? You'll move in when you graduate?"

"It's too much, though. I know you must have put hours and hours into fixing this up." She frowned again.

"It will never be enough."

"Harry, I do love the cottage. Tell you what though. I'll move into it under one condition, you'll make me one promise."

"What's that?"

"And I mean it Harry. I'm going to hold you to this promise."

He looked at the determined look on her face. "So, what is it?"

"You promise that you'll forgive yourself. That we're even now, even though I never thought it was your fault and you didn't need to make things *even*. If I so much as see the tiniest hint of guilt or pity in your eyes... even one time... I'll move out, sell it, and move away. I swear I will."

Harry drew in a long breath. Could he forgive himself and move on? Would he ever feel his debt was repaid?

"I honestly don't know if I can promise that, Rose. I'm always going to feel a responsibility towards you."

"I swear, if you can't get over feeling like you have to do things for me, that you owe me, I'll take my degree and move to the other end of the country."

"But, Rose, you said you want to come back here to Belle Island."

"I do. But not if I'm going to have to see you all the time and you're still playing the blame game. I can't live that way."

He looked at her for a long moment, the determined set of her shoulders, the way her eyes flashed with an I-mean-it-Harry look. "Okay, I'll try. I'll really try."

She reached out for him and he took her small hand in his. "This really is wonderful. I can't wait to finish up school and move in. I'm ready to start real life. I got such a late start to entering college. All those years of rehab before I was ready to go. Then it took me a few extra years to graduate. Between having to carefully plan out my courses so I didn't have back-to-back classes that were too far apart to get to on time, and changing my major, it's been a long haul."

"Well, I'm proud of you." Harry squeezed her hand.

"I'm kind of proud of myself, too. Now, how about you show me all around this place."

He showed her every little detail that he'd thought of to make things easier for her. The delight shining in her eyes was more than enough payment for all his hard work.

CHAPTER 12

Sammy entered the real estate office early the next morning after receiving a call from Jane Munson.

"Samantha, I have news for you." Jane motioned to a chair across from her desk. "The deed has been contested."

"Really?"

"It seems that many owners ago it was sold without one of the joint owners signing off on the sale. It was owned by a Phillip Thompson."

Sammy's world tilted off axis.

"I know that Thompson is a common name, but I know you're only interested in that specific cottage. Is he any relation to you?"

"I… He's… my father."

Jane looked up from the notes in front of her. "I see." Jane looked at her closely. "Let me get you some water. You look a little pale."

Jane came back with a cold bottle of water. Sammy slowly unscrewed the top and took a long drink. Her father? How had he come to own it? It was her *grandparents'* cottage. Her *mother's* parents.

"I don't understand…"

"It says here that Phillip Thompson bought it over forty years ago. He sold it about eighteen years ago. It's had a few owners, but a Shelly Thompson has a claim on it."

"My mother?" Sammy didn't think anything could surprise her more than finding out her father had owned the cottage. But this bit of information did.

"Shelly Thompson is your mother? She's filed that she was part owner when your father sold the cottage."

"My mother has *no right* to that cottage. None."

"According to the lawyer she's hired, she does have a valid claim."

"She disappears for twenty years, and now says she has a claim to the cottage. She does not. Not after what she did." The heat rose in Sammy's cheeks. There was no way that her mother was going to get that cottage. Not if Sammy had anything to say about it.

Then her mind circled back to the fact that her father had owned the cottage, not her grandparents like she'd thought. Nothing made sense. But her grandparents had loved the cottage. Had her father forced them to move after everything fell apart? Had he sold it out from under them?

There was no way around it, she was going to have to call him.

She stood up abruptly. "Thank you for all your hard work. I guess have I some calls to make. I'm still wanting to buy the property though, if we can get everything sorted out."

"It looks like it's a bit of a mess right now." Jane looked thoughtful. "Do you think you could talk to your mother and see what claim she has to the property?"

"I haven't spoken to my mother in twenty years and have no idea how to reach her." Sammy spun on her heels and hurried out the door, her mind whirling with questions.

~

That evening Sammy sat on the swing on the cottage porch, slowly swaying back and forth, wrapped in an afghan against the chilly night air. The sky was lit with stars like a sparkling diamond tiara showing off its brilliance.

She should have called her father, gotten things straightened out, and had him answer her questions. But she just wasn't ready for that conversation. Nor was she ready for his inevitable questions about the Adriana Boutiques account.

So much had happened in the week since she'd returned to Belle Island. She'd seen Harry again and he'd kissed her.

The kisses she was trying so hard to forget.

In spite of her best intentions, she'd fallen for him again. Which was a big mistake, because it was obvious he had a relationship with Rose. She pulled the wrap tightly around her shoulders and let out a long breath.

"Sams?" Harry's ever-so-familiar voice drifted across from the bottom of the deck stairs. "Can we talk?"

She swallowed. "I'm not sure we have anything to say."

"I think we do." He slowly climbed the steps and sat in the chair beside the swing. "You saw me with Rose."

"I did."

"But you ran off."

"No, I just decided I wasn't hungry." She lied right to his face. Then sighed. "Yes, I ran away."

"I'd like to explain." He leaned towards her.

She scooted further from him. "There's no need to explain. You don't owe me anything. Though, I wonder if your girlfriend would be happy to know you were kissing another woman."

"Sams, look at me." He reached out a hand and gently tilted her face towards him. "She's not my girlfriend. She *is* a friend, though. A good friend. And I feel a responsibility to... I don't know... to try and make her life easier."

Sammy looked into his face and saw the pain etched in his eyes. "Tally told me what happened."

Harry nodded. "Yes, Tally told me she'd talked to you and explained what happened. I wanted you to join us. To meet Rose. I think you'd both get along great."

Sammy's emotions swung in a roller coaster of highs and lows, not knowing how she felt about anything right now.

"Rose is a trooper. She's always looked at the bright side, even after life threw her this horrible curve. She's almost finished with college now. She'll be moving back to town."

"I see."

"I'll be glad to have her back here. She's my friend, Sams. Nothing more. We never were anything more than friends. I never had feelings for her like... not like I had for you. Like I *have* for you."

Sammy's heart pounded in her chest. He had feelings for her. Now.

"But I do feel responsible for Rose's accident. She never would have climbed that stupid waterslide if I hadn't dared her. We were always daring each other to do things. To stretch ourselves. To try new things. But this dare had terrible consequences. I should have gone up with her. Maybe I could have done something. If I could only take back those words, that dare."

"But you can't, can you?"

"No, I can't. And I feel like I've ruined her life."

"Oh, Harry. I know exactly how you feel. The need to take back words that you had no idea would have such far-reaching consequences." She reached over and took Harry's hand. "I want to tell you something."

"You know you can tell me anything."

"That night? That night after we went to the island and saw my mother?" Sammy drew in a deep breath. "How I reacted ruined everything."

"How was it that you think you ruined everything?"

"I sat at my grandparents' cottage, waiting for Mom to return. Then my father showed up to surprise us. I remember throwing myself into his arms, so glad to see him, so angry at my mother."

Sammy looked down and stared at her hands, fiddling with her watchband. "I was furious with my mother. She didn't know we had seen her and I wanted to hurt her for cheating on my father. I felt like she'd cheated on me, too, cheated on us as a family. So I did something really stupid. Right there in the middle of the living room with my father and my grandparents sitting there."

Harry sat quietly and let her continue. "My mother showed up a short time later. She went over and kissed my father. She kissed him. After spending the day with Jonathan. I was boiling mad. Spoiling for a fight with her. I wanted to hurt her, like she'd hurt my father, like *I* was hurting."

Sammy could still remember the feeling of uncontrolled rage and indignation that had surged through her. "Mom said she'd been out shopping all day. I remember my grandmother looking at my mother strangely, like she knew she was lying, too."

Sammy looked out at the ocean then back at Harry. "So I asked Mom how she got all that sunburn while she was shopping. She looked at me with such… surprise. There was a hint of fear in her eyes."

She scrubbed her hand over her face, the memories rushing back in a tidal wave of pain. "I handled it all wrong. *All wrong*. I asked her how Blue Heron Island had been and how Jonathan Eatherton was. Everyone turned to look at me. My grandmother shot me a look that said to please stop. My grandfather was totally confused. And my father… oh, my father's face. I'll never forget his expression."

"What happened then?" Harry's warm, low voice coaxed her to continue.

"My father turned, walked over to my mother, and looked her right in the eyes. His fists were balled up but I knew he'd never strike her. He just asked her if it was true."

A hot tear trailed down Sammy's cheek. "At first Mom just stood there with a look of fear in her eyes, not saying a word. Then she nodded yes. Dad turned to me and said I had five minutes to pack my suitcase and we were leaving. Mom started crying. My grandmother was crying. I ran to my room and threw things in my suitcase and Dad and I drove all night and the next day until we reached Chicago. That was the last time I saw my mother."

"She never tried to contact you?"

"She called off and on the first few years. Not often. I never spoke with her. Dad became even more driven at work. I went to business school so I could work with him. I felt I owed him that much."

She dashed away more tears. "I wish I'd kept my mouth shut. Maybe just confronted my mom by herself. Anything. I just didn't think. I should have known it would blow everything up. No more trips to the island, no more family holidays, no mother there for my graduations or to talk to. Dad divorced her so fast."

"Your mother was the one who cheated though." Harry reached over and stroked away a tear from her face.

"She did. I know that. But... if only I had just talked to her in private. Made her promise not to see Jonathan anymore. Or... something. I just miss the family life we had."

"I'm sorry you had such a rough time." Harry squeezed her hand. "You and your mother and father were gone the next day. I went to your grandparents' place first thing the next morning looking for you. I didn't know why you left without talking to me."

"Well, like I said, Dad and I left that night. We packed up our things and Father drove through the night to get us back home. I remember looking over at him just as daylight was dawning, the pale pink light hitting his ashen face. His face had a hardened look etched into it. A look that stayed there for a very long time. My father and I never spoke of it again."

"It all gets worse though." Unable to control them, tears streamed down her cheeks. "Mom and Jonathan left the island that night. My grandparents were angry with her, too. Right after the divorce went through and Mom wasn't covered by insurance, Jonathan and Mom were in a bad car accident. He was killed. She was hurt badly. My grandparents helped her out and got her in rehab, but spent most of their retirement on her medical bills. I thought that was why they sold the cottage, because they needed the money."

"It wasn't?"

"Now, I don't know. Today I found out my *father* owned the cottage. I always thought my grandparents did. Do you think he kicked them out to get back at my mom? I just don't know. He was so angry back then. I wouldn't put anything past him."

"Do you see your grandparents much?"

"Hardly ever. It's been years. At first they kept

trying to get me to see Mom. Then Mom was hurt and went to some rehab across the country. I was in college and well, last I heard she stayed out there. Somewhere in Seattle, I think. I felt like I would be betraying my father if I went to see her. My grandparents live in a retirement place near Orlando now."

She looked up at Harry. "So, you see. I understand wanting to take words back. To unsay things. And I thought that maybe, if I could get the cottage back for my grandparents, it would help… make amends… or *something*, for me destroying their lives."

He pulled her into his arms and held her close. "I see that you do understand, Sams. Words can have far reaching consequences. I'm so, so sorry."

Sammy leaned against him. "We're quite the pair, aren't we?"

Harry sat holding Sammy close against him. He stroked her hair, let her cry a bit more, then wiped away her tears. He'd had no idea that all that had happened after he'd left her that afternoon so long ago. No wonder she hadn't returned to Belle Island.

Sammy looked up at him, her eyes swollen from tears. "I need to call my father and ask some questions. I need to get my act together and present Adam with a plan for Hamilton Hotels. And I need to find a new place to stay, since I just rented this cottage for a week."

"Well, you're in luck there. The Andersons had it rented for a month—they rent it every year—but Mr. Anderson called. He said his wife is having medical problems, so they are staying home this winter. I'll let Lisa know you're staying longer."

"That would be so great. I really need to get all this sorted out."

He gave her a tentative smile. "So, that means you'll go out with me again?"

She made a valid attempt at returning his smile. "I'd like that. And I'd like to meet Rose, too."

"I'll set it up for before she heads back to college."

"Great."

"And I can tell you now why you can't buy Bellemire Cottage back for your grandparents."

"I still want to, Harry."

"I know, but it's impossible."

"Why is that?" She scrunched up her face.

"I didn't want to say anything before because I

had to show it to someone first. The cottage? It's Rose's cottage. I converted it for total wheelchair accessibility. She's going to move in this spring when she graduates."

"Oh…" Sammy's eyes clouded. "I so wanted to buy it back. But… it doesn't seem like that's going to happen now, does it? Not after you made it perfect for Rose. Why did you choose that cottage?"

"I'm sorry. I had no idea you'd ever want it, or that you'd ever come back to the island. I got a good deal on it for Rose."

Sammy let out a long, drawn-out sigh. "Well, it's not your fault. Even *I* didn't know I'd want to buy it. I just thought maybe I'd be able to fix things if I bought it. That maybe my mother might even visit my grandparents there. That maybe I'd be able to see her again." She shook her head. "That's a lot of maybes. Those were all just crazy dreams. It would probably make my father furious anyway."

"I'm sorry it turned out this way." He was sorry. In trying to do something nice for Rose, he'd prevented Sammy from getting what she needed.

Sammy looked at the ocean, then back to him. "Don't worry, Harry. We're all good."

Sammy smiled up at him and his heart soared with hope. Hope that maybe things would work out between them. At the very least he didn't want to lose her friendship again. And hope that maybe he could make peace with his past and what happened to Rose.

So much had happened in a week's time. Maybe his future was brighter than he thought.

CHAPTER 13

"I think I've tried on one hundred dresses." Julie stood in front of the full-length mirror at a bridal shop in Sarasota. Susan and Tally sat on a settee and watched as she turned this way and that. "I don't like this one, either."

"It is a bit fancier than I pictured as a dress for you." Tally nodded thoughtfully.

"Everything is fancier than what you'd picture me in. I'm not the glamorous type of gal." Julie stared at her reflection in the mirror. The dress made her look like someone's doll. She hated it. She hated every single dress she'd tried on. They all looked so modern and sleek. Many had low necklines or were strapless, which she hated. This particular one flared out from the knees in what the saleslady called a trumpet style. The last one had a sheer train from her shoulders and made her look like a bad attempt at a Greek goddess.

She hated them all.

But wouldn't Reed expect her to wear a proper wedding gown? He came from a wealthy family. One that was probably used to seeing brides in dresses that cost thousands of dollars. Or more.

"I'm pretty sure we haven't found the perfect dress for you yet." Susan screwed up her face and paused. "Maybe we're going about this all wrong."

"Well, I'm open to suggestions." Julie sighed.

"How about if we just find you a simple white dress to wear?"

"But... I'm afraid of disappointing Reed. He'll be expecting some kind of bridal gown."

"Reed would wed you in shorts and t-shirt. The man just wants to be married to you." Tally pushed off the brocade, tufted settee. "Enough of this. Susan is right. Go take off that gown."

"But, Reed..."

"Talk to the man. He loves you. You're the bride. Pick a dress you're happy with." Susan also stood. "And... words to live by... always listen to Tally."

Tally laughed.

Julie hurried back to the changing room to slip

out of the gosh-awful wedding gown, freeing herself from yards of chiffon and lace.

Now, she just had to face Reed... and his dreams of a fancy, proper wedding.

That evening Tally bustled around Magic Cafe, seating people, refilling water, making sure everything was taken care of. Same thing she did every day, but she never seemed to tire of it. She loved the restaurant, loved Belle Island, and enjoyed interacting with her customers. Some were regular island residents, some were annual snowbirds who came for the winter, always remarking how glad they were to be back.

She looked up and saw Josephine and Paul Clark entering the outside seating area. She hurried over. "So great to see you. You two don't usually come this late in the evening."

"Paul had a showing at the gallery that ran long. Then we decided we were starving." Josephine smiled.

"I can fix that." Tally smiled back at her friends. "Right this way."

"If things slow down, you want to join us?" Paul asked as he pulled out the chair for his wife.

"Let me get a few things wrapped up, and I will. I ate early tonight, but I'll join you for a bit anyway." Tally motioned for Tereza and hurried off to do her chores, so she could join her friends.

Right as Josephine and Paul were finishing their dinner, she slipped into a chair at their table, a glass of wine in her hand.

"Good, I'm glad you could join us." Josephine took a sip of her ice water.

"How did the showing at the gallery go?" Tally stretched out her legs, glad to be off her feet for a while.

"It went well. Had more people than we thought. Julie made us hors d'oeuvres and every single one was gone by the end. She's hired a girl to serve at events now, too." Paul pushed his dinner plate aside, every bit of food eaten.

"I heard she'd done that. Smart move on her part. She's turned into a sharp businesswoman." Tally nodded her head. "Too bad she can't make a decision about her wedding dress. The shopping trip today was kind of a disaster. She wants simple, but still have a wedding feel to the dress."

Josephine leaned forward. "You know my grandniece, Bella, right? I talked to her today and she said she'd found some lovely vintage wedding dresses for her shop. I could see if she would send a few down here for Julie to look at. I'll ask if she has something simple."

"That would be great. I could see Julie in something simple and vintage." Tally figured if she didn't do something soon, Julie would be walking down the aisle naked as a jaybird.

"I'll talk to her tomorrow first thing." Josephine looked pleased.

The three sat and chatted for another fifteen minutes or so until Josephine smothered a yawn. "Oh, I'm sorry. I'm getting tired, I guess."

Paul stood and pulled out Josephine's chair. "My Jo has never been much of a late night girl. I think it's time to take her home."

Josephine stood and she and Paul walked out of the cafe, hand in hand. Tally smiled as she watched them go. So in love after so very many years. They were lucky. Very lucky. Not many people got that.

Tally gathered up a handful of the dishes from the table and went inside to finish up some bookwork before calling it a night herself. She just hoped she'd managed to solve Julie's wedding dress dilemma with help from Bella.

CHAPTER 14

Sammy had spent a few days perfecting her promotional plans for the Hamilton Hotels and avoiding her father's phone calls. She'd let his administrative assistant know she was staying longer and working not only on the Adriana Boutique account, but on a new client. She told his assistant she'd be back in Chicago within a week.

She wanted to talk to her father and ask him about owning Bellemire, but she didn't want to upset him. They never talked about that night all those years ago. Never talked about her mother. Never talked about anything that came before that night. It was like that life had never existed. Asking him about ownership of the cottage would break their tacit agreement.

Plus, she knew she was avoiding talking to him about the Adriana account. She wanted one more shot at the account before admitting defeat. That meeting was set up for tomorrow. She stared at her computer screen with the presentation slides.

She was proud of the plans she came up with for the hotels but still unsure on the Adriana Boutiques presentation. Part of the problem with the shop was that they weren't really sure what they wanted. Sammy had done some focus groups and target market research on who their customers were, but Adriana wasn't sure that was truly their market.

Her phone rang, and she glanced at it to make sure it wasn't her father before answering it. Harry.

"Hi." She pushed back from the table where she'd spread out her work.

"I know it's last minute, but do you want to go to Magic Cafe tonight for dinner? It's Rose's last night in town before she heads back to college. I swear, she'd love to eat at Magic Cafe every night she's in town. Does dinner work for you?"

"That works. I'll meet you guys there?"

"Sure. About five-thirty? Then we should be able to catch the sunset, unless it storms."

"Five-thirty it is." She clicked off the phone and stood, stretching her arms above her head, then flexing her shoulders up and down. She really should remember to take breaks when she worked so many hours at the computer.

Sammy speculated about what Rose was like. She couldn't help but wonder that even though Harry insisted there was nothing between him and Rose... maybe there was. Maybe she'd spot something when she saw them together. Or maybe Harry was clueless that Rose had a thing for him.

She cocked her head to one side then the other, reaching up to rub her neck. She snatched a sweater and walked outside. The wind whipped across the deck and storm clouds threatened in the distance. She wasn't used to chilly weather on Belle Island. She'd always come down in the summertime. Still, this weather was much better than the eighteen inches of snow Chicago had gotten in the last two days. Much better than that.

She stood staring out at the waves, knowing she'd miss this view when she returned home. Now that she'd finally come back to visit the island, she'd miss it when she left. She'd miss the island and so much more.

She'd miss Harry.

Harry didn't know why he was so nervous, but he

was. He looked at his khaki slacks making sure they didn't look wrinkled. He'd grabbed a light sweater because he was sure, unless the weather turned downright ugly, Rose would want to sit outside at the cafe. He took one last look in the mirror—*what was wrong with him this evening*—and headed out the door.

Rose was waiting by her front door. "I'm driving."

"Of course you are." Harry smiled at her. "Like that new freedom, don't you?"

"You have no idea. I can go where I want, when I want. I don't have to rely on other people to take me, or taxis, or Uber, or bus schedules." She grinned at him. "Plus it's red. I love everything about it."

They got in the car and Rose looked over at him sitting in the passenger seat. She cocked her head to one side. "You look nice."

"Um, thanks?"

"So, I'm going to meet the famous Sammy."

"I think you two will like each other."

"Any friend of yours is a friend of mine." Rose started at him for a moment. "Hey, you look... nervous. I swear you do."

"No I don't."

"Harry Moorehouse. You've fallen for Sammy again, haven't you?"

"I don't know what you're talking about."

Rose laughed. "Nope, you have. I can see it plainly on your face. Heck, anyone could see it."

"No, we're just friends. Besides, she's only in town for a few more days."

"Right, Harry. Whatever you say." She rolled her eyes.

Rose never was one to let him get away with anything, but he wasn't about to admit that he had feelings for Sammy again. And he wanted the two women to get along. They were both important people in his life.

He frowned. Sammy *was* an important person in his life again, that much he could admit. Rose turned the ignition and the car roared to life. Rose sighed and he laughed at her.

"I love this car." She grinned, pulled out of the parking space, and they headed to the cafe.

Tally walked up as Harry and Rose entered the cafe. "Rose, you going to come here every night?" Tally smiled at them.

"I'm headed back out of town tomorrow, so this will have to hold me for a while."

"You two want inside or out? I have the patio heaters going outside, so it's really pretty nice out there. Looks like we're in for a pretty sunset with those storm clouds clearing out."

"Let's sit outside, Harry. You think that will be okay with Sammy?"

"I'm sure it will be." Harry was certain that Sammy would dress to sit outside. She was just like Rose in that way. They both loved to be outside when they were on the island.

They got situated at the table and ordered their drinks. When his beer arrived, Harry took a long swallow. Rose looked at him and grinned. "So, what are you so nervous about? Afraid I won't like her? Or afraid she won't like me?"

Harry raked his hand through his hair. "I have no idea, Rose. I'm just… antsy or something."

"Or something." She flashed him what-am-I-going-to-do-with-you look.

He stood and waved when he spotted Sammy come out on the patio. She looked… beautiful. She wore a pair of black slacks and a pink sweater. She'd caught her hair back in some kind of tieback thingie. She made her way to their table.

He swallowed and rubbed his hand on his

slacks. He reached out to take her hand as she got to the table. "Sammy, I want you to meet Rose. Rose, this is Sammy."

"I've heard so much about you, Sammy. It's nice to meet you." Rose was perfectly charming, but it didn't fool him. She was checking Sammy out.

"It's nice to meet you, too, Rose."

He held out a chair, and Sammy slipped into it. He sat down and waved to their waitress. Sammy ordered a drink, and an awkward silence fell over the table. Sammy's drink arrived and she took a slow sip of it.

"Oh, for goodness sake." Rose rolled her eyes. "Harry here has been so nervous about us meeting. What's up with that?"

Sammy cocked her head to one side. "Harry *is* charming, but he does have his quirks."

"Right, doesn't he?" Rose grinned at Sammy. "Like that little twitch at the side of his mouth when he's not quite telling you the whole story."

"Oh, you noticed that, too?" Sammy winked at Rose. "How about how he always clears his throat before he gets ready to tell you something he thinks you don't want to hear?"

"Right. Like that." Rose studied Harry for a moment. "But, like you said, he's charming."

"I'm sitting right here, you know. You two

about finished up dissecting me?" Harry looked from Rose to Sammy, not sure that introducing them was his smartest move.

"Oh, I'm sure we'll have lots more to compare notes on, don't you worry." Sammy's words came across with a laughing, fake-soothing tone.

Harry sighed. "I'm sure you will."

Sammy sat on her deck late that evening enjoying a glass of wine, the moon shining on the ocean, and the stars dancing in the sky. She'd had a wonderful time at Magic Cafe. Rose was witty, fun, and delightful. She seemed independent and full of life, of course Harry would like her.

Sammy had to admit that she was relieved to see no hint from Rose that she had any greater feelings for Harry other than good friends.

Not that Sammy had any right to be jealous. She'd disappeared on Harry long ago and he was entitled to have any relationship he wanted with another woman.

And yet…

The thought of Harry with someone else made her heart ache. She needed to turn that feeling off, because even if she and Harry had made some kind of tentative truce this week, her life was back in Chicago. She didn't have summers free to come back and relive her past. They'd both moved on.

"Hey, Sams." Harry climbed the stairs to the deck. "I saw your lights were still on. Mind if I join you for a bit?"

Or maybe they *hadn't* moved on...

"Of course. There's a bottle of red wine inside if you'd like to have a glass, or there's beer in the fridge."

Harry disappeared inside and came back out with the wine bottle and a glass. She watched his strong, tanned hands as he poured himself a glass, took a sip, and settled back on the chair beside her.

A shiver ran through her and she pulled her wrap tightly around her. Though, she didn't think the shiver was from the cool night air...

A cloud slipped over the moon and dropped them into darkness.

"Did you have a good time tonight?" Harry's low voice enveloped her like the afghan, warming her, yet making her shiver again.

There was something so intimate sitting here in the shadows with Harry. Close enough to touch him— yet, she wouldn't, couldn't.

"Sams?"

What had he asked her? Oh, yes, about tonight. "I

had a great time. Rose is really nice. She's funny and I can see why you're friends with her."

"She has been a great friend. I'm glad you two hit it off, even if you did pick on me."

She could hear the teasing in his voice. "Well, you decided we should meet, so it's all on you."

"Big mistake on my part. Really big." Harry's laugh drifted across the mere feet between them. So close.

His warm hand covered her hand resting on the arm of the Adirondack chair. An instant heat spiked up her arm, flushing her with longing. A longing for Harry's kiss.

As if he could read her mind, he leaned over and kissed her gently. Her hand slid up his arm then rested on his chest. His heart beat strongly, wildly under her palm pressed against him.

"Mmmm." His word was more a growl than a word. He pulled back slightly. "I do like kissing you."

"I pretty much enjoy it myself." She smiled at him.

"Then I think I should kiss you again."

She leaned forward. "I think you should."

After kissing her thoroughly he pulled back again. "Sams, those feelings I had for you all those years ago?"

She nodded.

"Well, I think they are all coming back. Or maybe they never left."

The moonlight flooded over them again, and she could clearly see the sincerity in his eyes. Sincerity and longing. A longing and desire that seemed to match her own.

"I…" What could she answer? That she cared about him, too? That his kisses made all her problems go away and all she could think about was him? But, she knew she had to choose her words carefully. She'd at least learned that lesson very well.

"Harry, I've probably always cared about you. Never quite forgotten you, even when I was miles away. But…"

"But what?"

"But, we're different now. Not those kids. We have separate lives in separate cities. Long distance relationships—if you are talking about a relationship with me— bring their own set of problems." Sammy looked down at her hands. "Besides, this is too fast. Nothing good comes from jumping into things."

"So, you don't even want to try and see where this is going?" His voice was tinged with hurt.

"I could never leave my father's company. Never desert him. Your business is here. So, really, there is no point to all this, is there?" She'd never hurt her father again. Ever. She raised her eyes to look at Harry.

"No point?" Harry looked directly into her eyes.

"Can't we just enjoy this time we have together now? Enjoy each other's company? I don't even know if I'll be here more than a few more days." Besides, she needed time to think. And how could he want to be with her? She ruined things for the people she loved. He knew that.

Wait, had she just admitted to herself that she had feelings for him?

"That's all you want from me, Sams? Are you sure?"

She wasn't sure about much of anything, but she *was* positive she'd never put Harry in a position where she could hurt him. And she could never abandon her father. "I think that's all we have, Harry."

He pushed off his chair and handed her his half-empty wine glass. "That's not enough for me, I want more."

He turned and trudged down the deck stairs and off down the beach, disappearing in the distance as another cloud cloaked the moon and plunged her into darkness.

CHAPTER 15

The next day her presentation to Adriana went better than she'd expected, which was surprising, because all she could think about was Harry and what he said. Harry still cared about her and just seeing her this week wasn't enough for him.

Did *she* want more? Her thoughts whirled around in her brain, making her want to scream or race down the beach or just do *something* to stop the thinking. She was always over thinking every single decision she ever made anymore.

And she couldn't get the picture out of her mind of him walking away down the beach.

She pushed her thoughts of Harry far from her mind and back on business. Or at least she pretended to.

Maybe she would still win the Adriana account. That would make her father happy. She hated to lose the first account that he'd let her handle and present on her own.

She walked back and forth, pacing the floor in the small cottage. She also wanted to tweak the promotion for Hamilton Hotels. Something was just not quite right, but she couldn't put her finger on it.

Nine steps across the room, turn, nine steps back. She chewed her lower lip, considering ideas, one by one, then tossing each one aside.

A knock at the door brought her from her thoughts and she glanced at her watch. Four o'clock. She crossed the floor and pulled open the door, hoping it wasn't Harry—or hoping it was.

She blinked against the sudden light, then caught her hand on the doorframe, steadying herself. A gasp escaped her lips. She wasn't sure if she was seeing a ghost or having a dream or... *was this real?*

"Samantha."

"M-mom." She could barely choke out the word.

They stood, frozen. Sammy slowly looked at her, this woman who had been out of her life for twenty years. Her mother looked older. Her hair was gray now and cut in a stylish short cut. She was dressed in casual but classic clothes, with sunglasses perched upon her head.

"What are you doing here? How did you find me?" Sammy couldn't take her eyes off her mother, but didn't invite her in.

Her mother was doing a good job of staring, too. "I was on the island on business and found out you were here. It's still a small town. Didn't take me long to find out where you were staying."

"What business could you possibly have on the island?"

Her mother ignored the question. "You look so... beautiful. All grown up."

"What business?" Sammy ignored her mother's comment.

"Just a little problem that never got settled. I'm handling it. Are you going to ask me in?"

"So after twenty years you're just going to show up and you want me to say 'sure, that's fine, come on in'?"

"I tried to keep in touch with you. Tried to see you. At first your father blocked every attempt."

"Gosh, I wonder why." Sammy heard the cold, sarcastic tone of her words. Though, her heart fluttered a bit. Her mother had come to find her. To see her. She stomped that feeling flat, ignoring it.

"Please, Samantha, can we talk?"

"I'm pretty sure there's nothing to say."

Her mother reached out for Sammy's hand resting on the doorjamb with the lightest of a caress. Sammy stared at their two hands touching, *touching* after all these years.

Sammy snatched her hand away, ignoring the momentary warmth of her mother's touch, and said nothing.

"I'll be here in town for a few days. I'm staying at Belle Island Inn if you change your mind. I hope you'll decide to come see me. I really want a chance for us to talk." Her mother's eyes searched Sammy's face, obviously looking for some hint of acceptance.

Sammy gave her none.

Her mother turned and walked away. Sammy stood in stony silence, afraid to speak. Wanting to stop her mother—yet she didn't. Sammy closed the door and leaned against it. She slowly slid down to the floor, sat on the sandy doormat, and buried her face in her hands.

Sammy stood at the window, watching the sun set over the slow rolling waves. The day ended in a kaleidoscope of intertwining colors. The riotousness of the sunset matched her mood. Unsettled, ever changing.

Like magic, Harry appeared at the French door on the deck. Why? Hadn't they said all that needed to be said?

She couldn't hide from him, so she slowly opened the door. "What do you want?"

"I came to check on you. I heard your mother was back in town." Harry's eyes conveyed the same concern she heard in his voice.

"She is. She stopped by." Sammy stepped back to let Harry enter, because all of a sudden she couldn't bear to be alone. Harry slipped into the room, passing inches from her.

"Are you okay?" He reached out to touch her.

She wanted to jerk away from his touch, her emotions were so raw. But she also wanted to tumble into his arms and be comforted. She wanted... she didn't know what she wanted.

But Harry did. He pulled her into his muscular arms—that somehow felt so gentle—and held her close, stroking her hair with consoling murmurs. She let herself relax into his embrace, glad to have someone here with her, glad to take strength from him.

She finally pulled away from him and walked

over to the sofa. Harry followed her and sat beside her.

"Do you want to tell me what happened when she came to see you?"

Sammy looked down and fiddled with her watch. "She wanted to talk. But I was so shocked. I cut her off. I didn't let her come in."

"You had every right to be shocked."

"All that anger came welling back. That she cheated on my father, cheated on us as a family."

Harry nodded and let her continue.

"But, you know what? There was this part of me, this tiny part of me, that was so glad to see her. It was like I was a little girl again and so glad to be seeing my mom, and all the bad stuff was gone." She shoved her hair away from her face and sighed. "But, of course, none of it's gone. It's all still right there."

She stood and started pacing the floor. "She's staying at the inn for a few days. She wants me to come see her and talk."

"Do you want to?"

"I… I just don't know. Part of me does. Part of me wants to ignore her and hurt her back. I feel like she deserted me." She stopped pacing and turned to look directly at Harry. "And a big part of me is afraid of disappointing my father if he finds out I met with her. I couldn't bear to hurt him."

"You know, Sams, I think in this case you need to do what is right for *you*. All three of you are adults now. You're not purposely hurting your father. It's okay to want to see your mom again after all this time. Maybe it will help you make peace with the past."

"I…" Her voice dropped to a whisper. "I just miss my mom so much. No matter what happened. I miss her." She rubbed her temples. "I need time to think this through, make sure no one gets hurt."

"Sams, sometimes you just have to jump in and trust your gut. Do you want to see her?"

Sammy nodded slowly.

"Then, I think the decision is made."

"I guess it is." Sammy sat beside Harry. "I'll go see her tomorrow."

Harry pulled her against him and tucked her by his side. He draped an arm around her and they sat like that for a very long time, the warmth of his body a soothing balm to her turbulent nerves.

She rested her head against him, wishing she could stay here all night. His calm to her storm. As darkness descended, Harry finally loosened his hold and slid away from her on the sofa. "You going to be okay?" His voice was low and questioning.

"I think so." Actually she had no idea if she was going to be okay, but she couldn't quite bring herself to tell him that.

"I'll go now, then. You can call me if you need to talk."

Sammy nodded. Harry stood and brushed a hand along her cheek, then turned and slipped out the door. Tonight was just like Harry. Harry the friend. He was there when she needed him, even though she couldn't give him what he needed in return.

She sat in the darkness. Alone. Confused. And wishing she'd asked Harry to stay with her.

Harry trudged back to Bellemire. There was nothing that would have kept him away from Sammy tonight after he'd heard her mother was in town. He had to see her. To make sure she was okay. He wanted to protect her and make her life easier. He wanted…

He kicked at the sand then looked up at the stars.

He wanted Sammy in his life. He wanted Sammy to want *him*.

CHAPTER 16

Sammy walked into Belle Island Inn the next morning determined to find her mother. She'd finally admitted there was no way she could keep away from her mom, not when they were this close. She paused as she entered, then strode over to the reception desk.

An older lady looked up and smiled at her. "May I help you?"

"I… I'm looking for my mother. She's staying here."

"Her name?" The lady's hands poised over the keyboard of the computer.

"Ah… Shelly Thompson."

The lady clicked away at the keys and looked

up. "I'm sorry, I don't see anyone with that name registered."

Sammy chewed her lip. "Shelly Eatherton?" Had her mom and Jonathon gotten married before he died? She had no idea.

"No…" The woman eyed her for a moment.

"She's about my height, short gray hair."

The woman looked closely at Sammy. "There's a woman who looks just like you staying here. I mean, you look just like her. She has to be your mother."

Sammy caught her breath. No one had said that to her in a long, long time. She used to hear it often, how much she and her mother looked alike.

"I think I saw her head out to the deck not too long ago." The woman smiled at her and nodded to the door to the deck.

"Thank you." Sammy headed outside.

She saw her mother perched on a high chair, staring out at the ocean. The breeze ruffled her short hair. Her mother looked up and watched a pelican swoop by overhead. Memories rained down on her, ones she'd ignored for so long. The times she and her mother would go sit on the beach and watch the birds. Swimming in the waves with her mother and grandparents. Walking on the beach talking to her mother about anything and everything.

She started across the planks of the deck, slowly making her way over to her mother, drawn by an invisible magnet.

Her mother turned just as she reached her. "Samantha, you came."

"I… I couldn't *not* come."

Her mother smiled. Ah, how she'd missed her mother's smile.

"Here, why don't you sit by me." Her mother patted a chair next to her.

Sammy climbed on the chair and sat looking out at the ocean, not sure what to say.

"I'm really glad you came. I've missed you so much. I… I'm sorry. I can't even begin to tell you how sorry I am. I didn't mean to ruin everything." Her mother's voice was low. "I was just… so lonely with your father. That's no excuse, I know that. I'm not making an excuse. Just explaining how it happened. It shouldn't have happened, though. I should have kept trying to get your father to… I don't know. I wanted him to need me, want to spend time with me."

"That's your excuse?" Sammy scowled at her mother. She was still angry with her…but, ah, it was so good to see her.

"No, it's not an excuse. There was no excuse for

tearing our family apart. I was unfaithful. It's unforgivable. I'm so sorry it blew up your life."

"I wish I'd never seen you and Jonathan. Things would have been so different. I wish..." What did she wish? Would they just have gone on how they were? A pretend family? Would her mother have been content to just exist for all these years? Sammy knew her father didn't spend much time with her mom. Not like when she'd been really young. He'd gotten busy and forgotten birthdays and anniversaries. Sometimes he never made it down to Belle Island in the summertime to visit them. Now, as an adult, she could see how unhappy her mother had been back then.

Her mother sat silently watching her.

"I wish I wouldn't have blurted everything out that night. That I would have talked to you. I was just so angry and Dad showed up and..."

"It wasn't your fault. It was too much for you, I understand. It was *my* fault. *My* mistake. We all paid the price. I'll never forgive myself. I've missed so much of your life. I did see you graduate from college, though. I went to the ceremony and stood in the back. I was so proud of you, graduating with honors."

Sammy looked at her mother in surprise. "You were there?"

Her mother nodded and reached out to cover Sammy's hand.

Sammy looked down at their hands, mother and daughter, and a sob welled up. "Mom... I... I've missed you so much."

Her mother stood and put her arms around Sammy. A warmth filled her soul as only a mother's hug can. "I've missed you too, sweetheart. So much."

Sammy walked with her mother into the lobby. A storm was quickly approaching and had chased them inside. Adam entered the lobby and waved when he saw them.

"Samantha. What brings you to the inn?"

"Adam, this is my mother, Shelly. She's staying here at the inn for a few days."

"Very nice to meet you Mrs. Thompson."

"Oh, it's Shelly Werner."

Sammy looked at her mother in surprise. Her mom had taken back her maiden name.

"But just call me Shelly."

"Will do." Adam turned to Sammy. "So are you ready to present your ideas for the Hamilton Hotel promotion?"

"I am." Well, she still thought something was a bit wrong, but couldn't figure it out. But she would.

"How about tomorrow afternoon? Does that work with your schedule?"

"Yes, tomorrow is fine." She'd make it fine even if she had to stay up all night and finalize her presentation.

"Great. About two?"

"That works."

The woman from the reception desk hurried up to them. "Adam, have you seen your mother?"

"Dorothy, no, I just got here. Why?"

"I was supposed to meet Mary here and we were going to the knitting club at the yarn shop."

"You looked in her room?"

"She's not there."

Another woman entered the lobby. Adam turned to her. "Susan, have you seen Mom?"

"Not since this morning."

Adam frowned.

The woman reached out her hand. "Hi, I'm Susan, Adam's wife. I run the inn with Jamie, my son. I think you know him, right?"

Sammy shook the woman's hand. "I do know Jamie. This is my mom, Shelly Werner."

"I met you when you were checking in. Glad to

have you staying with us." Susan turned to Adam. "So, you're looking for Mary?"

"She was supposed to meet Dorothy to go to their knitting group." Adam's voice held an edge of concern.

Sammy could see the look of unease that passed between Susan, Dorothy, and Adam. "Is everything all right?"

"Not sure." Adam frowned again. "Maybe we could all split up and see if we can find her."

Susan turned to Sammy and her mother. "Adam's mother has Alzheimer's and has been a bit more confused these days. We're worried she might wander off and have a hard time finding her way back to the inn."

"Can we help?" Sammy's mom offered.

"I…" Adam raked his hand through his hair. "Yes, that would be great."

CHAPTER 17

Adam yanked out his cell phone, scrolled through his photos, and showed Sammy and Shelly a picture of his mom.

This was probably nothing. She'd probably gone for a walk and just lost track of time. Right? That was all it was.

Or she was lost…

His heart hammered in his chest, mocking his attempt to stay calm. He knew his mother wanted to retain what independence she could, but he was constantly worried that her Alzheimer's would get the better of her. It broke his heart to think of her out there and too confused to find her way home.

Maybe that *was* what happened. Maybe she was lost and couldn't find her way back. Maybe living on the island was too new and different for her. So many maybes.

Susan rested her hand on his arm. "I'm going to call Jamie. He's just in town. We'll get everyone looking for her."

Susan snatched her phone from her pocket and tapped on it to call Jamie. A frown crossed her face. "He's not answering."

"It looks like the storm is going to be here soon." Adam bit his lip. "We need to find her. Do you think she went out walking? Went into town? Out on the beach? I don't know where to start."

"Dorothy, why don't you and Shelly head down the beach?" Susan quickly took charge. "Adam, we'll take the car up to Lighthouse Point and look both directions that way."

"Samantha, can you head into town? I think Jamie was going to lunch at either The Lucky Duck or the Sweet Shoppe. Could you see if you can find him? And ask around about Mary while you're there?"

"Yes, I'd be glad to. I have Adam's cell phone number. I'll call if I find out anything."

Adam looked at Susan, grateful she'd taken control. He'd never forgive himself if something happened to his mother. He'd been just going along

COTTAGE NEAR THE POINT

with her, not taking the precautions that he should have taken. Things were going to change.

But first they needed to find his mom.

"Let's go." He hurried out of the lobby, trying to convince himself Susan's quickly thought-out plan would work, they'd find his mother before the storm hit, and that she'd be safe and sound.

Oh, why hadn't he thought to put some kind of GPS locator— a bracelet or something on her? He swore he'd be a better son, take better care of her, if only they could find her and she was unharmed.

Sammy drove into town and parked her car by the Lucky Duck. She glanced up and down the street, but didn't see anyone who looked even close to the photo Adam had shown her. She hurried through the door of the tavern and waited a moment for her eyes to adjust to the subtle lighting. She took another step into the room, looking all around for Jamie.

The door squeaked open behind her and she moved to the side to get out of the way.

"Sams." Harry's deep voice came from behind her.

She turned to look at him. Harry had always

had a knack for appearing when she needed him. "Harry, have you seen Jamie?"

Harry's forehead crinkled and he glanced around the tavern. "I'm meeting him here for lunch. He isn't here yet?"

"Not yet."

The door swung yet again and Jamie entered.

"Jamie. Your mother is looking for you." Sammy stepped forward and touched Jamie's arm. "Adam's mother is missing. Susan wants you to help look for Mary. They're worried because the storm is coming in quickly."

Jamie snatched his phone from his pocket and looked at it. "Darn it. Had it on silent. He flipped it on and played a voice message from his mom.

"Your mom wanted you to look around town. She and Adam went to Lighthouse Point, and Dorothy and my mom are looking on the beach by the inn."

"Okay, I'll call and let her know you found me. Gotta go, Harry. Another time."

"Hey, we'll help. How about we go look on the bay side beach area?"

"Thanks, buddy. Call if you find her."

All three of them hurried out the door. Sammy and Harry headed down Oak Street, past the live oak and the gazebo, and crossed to the beach. She looked up at the darkening sky with ugly blue-black clouds threatening to let loose with all the anger of a passionate, jilted lover. Or the fury of an angry daughter... She pushed her thoughts away.

Harry grabbed her hand and they hurried out onto the long stretch of beach that ran along the bay.

"Should we split up?" Sammy looked left and right.

"I don't really want to leave you alone with this storm approaching. Let's both head this way towards the pier."

Thunder roared overhead and lightening crackled through the sky. They raced down the beach, hand in hand. Sammy stumbled and crashed against Harry. He caught her before she fell and held her for a moment while she steadied herself. "You okay?"

"I'm fine." Her words came out in gasps. She bent over to catch her breath. "Okay, let's go."

The bay was covered in waves now, looking more like the seaside than bayside. Rain began to pelt them as they raced for the pier. The sky let loose, drenching them. Harry pulled her to the relative safety of a spot under the pier, and she bent over again, gasping for breath.

She finally caught her breath and stood. Harry

wrapped his arms around her providing protection from the storm. She shivered against him. She refused to think about how cold she was, drenched from the rain. All she could concentrate on was Mary out in this storm.

~

The storm would not cooperate and the heavens opened and pelted rain down on Adam and Susan as they hurried along the beach by Lighthouse Point. He couldn't help but think there was something he could have done to prevent this. Made sure someone was always watching his mom and hired her a companion. Heck, at this point he *almost* wished he'd locked her in her room when he couldn't be with her. Anything to keep her safe.

Was she standing out in the rain, confused and frightened? Had she gone into the ocean? Forgotten how to swim? Gotten knocked over by a wave? His mind raced from one horrible scenario to the next.

He clenched his jaw and held firmly to Susan's hand. He should get Susan out of the storm and to safety, too. "Let me get you inside somewhere."

"Not leaving you. Let's keep looking."

"But—"

"Don't argue with me. I'd never leave you. Let's find Mary."

They got close to the Lighthouse when it started to hail. His heart clenched in his chest. Was his mother out in this? Had she found shelter? The thought of hail hammering down on his mother tore at his heart.

"Come on. Let's go under the walkway to the lighthouse while it's hailing." His words were barely audible over the howling of the storm.

They ducked under the walkway to escape the worst of the storm. Susan shivered beside him as they crawled beneath the low walkway.

"Hi, honey." His mother's voice came from close by, loud enough to be heard over the pounding storm.

Adam looked up in surprise. Mary sat cross-legged on the sand under the walkway.

"Mom." Adam's heart swelled and relief washed over him. He crawled over to his mom. "You're safe."

"Of course I am. I just popped under here to get out of the storm. It came up so quickly."

"I was so worried about you." He scanned her to see if she was okay. She looked drier than he and Susan were.

"Adam, dear, there is no need for you to get so worried about me all the time."

"Yes, there is, Mom. You have Alzheimer's. We both know that. I worry that you'll get lost." His words came out harsher than he meant. He wasn't usually so blunt about her disease. "Why didn't you turn back when you saw the storm headed in?"

"I had to save this little guy…" Mary opened her jacket and a small furry head popped out. "Poor little thing was lost and all alone out here on the beach. Then he ran and I had to chase him. I think he thought we were playing a game." Mary smiled.

A small cavalier puppy with big, soulful eyes stared at Adam. Adam refused to be won over.

"Why didn't you call when you saw you couldn't make it back to safety in time?" Adam scowled at the puppy who had caused all this trouble and then scowled at his mother for good measure.

"I'm sorry, son. But it seems like in my chasing of the puppy, I lost my phone. Must have fallen out of my pocket."

"Ah, Mom." A long breath whooshed out of his lungs and he hugged his mother *and* the blasted puppy. The puppy let out a startled bark.

Susan crawled up behind him. "Well, if that isn't the cutest puppy I've ever seen"

"No, he's not." Adam scowled again.

"Yes, he is, son. Susan is right. You should always listen to your wife." Mary grinned.

Adam was outnumbered and knew when to throw in the towel. "Okay, okay. We'll stay here until the storm passes, then we'll head back home. I'll call everyone and let them know we found you."

"I wasn't lost, son."

Adam turned his back and rolled his eyes. One thing was for certain. This would never happen again.

CHAPTER 18

"Okay, thanks, buddy. Glad they found her." Harry clicked off his phone and wrapped his arms around Sammy again. She shivered against him. He needed to get her home and warm.

"They found Mary?"

"Yes, she was under the boardwalk by the lighthouse. It seems she was out rescuing a puppy."

"Thank goodness." Sammy voice was filled with relief.

"I need to get you warmed up."

"I'm f-fine."

"Right. I can tell by the way you can barely get your words out between your chattering teeth."

He looked up at the sky. "It looks like the worst is over. The hail stopped. If we cut down this side street across the island, we'll be pretty near your cottage. You up for a run for it?"

"Well, at least running might w-warm me up." She chattered.

He grabbed her hand tightly in his. "Okay, let's go."

They raced across the island and finally stumbled into Sammy's cottage. He immediately went to her bathroom and turned the shower on full force. "Strip and get in there and warm up. I'll make some coffee."

Sammy's hands shook as she tried to unbutton her sweater. He deftly undid the buttons for her, shucked the wet garment, and tossed it aside. Her t-shirt and jeans clung to her, but he ignored it. He turned his back. "You okay, now?"

"Thanks, Harry. Here take some towels from the linen closet to dry off."

He grabbed the offered towels and walked out of the bathroom, closing the door firmly behind him.

Though, he'd really like to climb right in that hot shower with her…

Clean up your thoughts, mister.

He hurried to her kitchen and started a big pot of coffee. He shivered as he worked and decided his best course of action would be to get into dry clothes. Only, he didn't have any, of course. He walked to the small laundry room and pulled off his jeans and shirt. They stuck to him like a second skin, refusing to be peeled. He wrestled with them, won the battle, and threw them in the dryer. He wrapped a towel around his waist and padded back into the kitchen.

Her shivering finally subsided in the rush of the deliciously hot shower. Sammy wasn't sure how long she stood under the steamy spray before she reluctantly turned off the water and stepped out. The bathroom was fogged over with steam, and she swiped a towel along the mirror. The tantalizing aroma of coffee drifted into the room as she towel-dried her hair. She went into her bedroom and pulled on dry jeans and a heavy sweater. She started out of the room, but with a second thought, she reached into her suitcase and got out a pair of socks. She tugged them on and slipped on a pair of sneakers. With a quick look in the mirror, she headed for the kitchen and the hot coffee.

She stopped in her tracks when she entered the kitchen. Harry stood at the kitchen sink, staring out the window. He was naked down to his towel-clad waist. His broad shoulders and muscled arms accentuated his narrow waist. She smothered a gasp.

He must have heard her though, because he turned slowly around. He stared back at her. There was no denying the hungry look in his eyes, they blazed with desire.

"I… uh…" She just stood staring at him like a fool.

"I threw my clothes in the dryer."

"I—I can see that."

"Hope that's okay."

Sure, it's perfectly fine to have a half-naked man in the kitchen and I'm going to just act like it's an everyday occurrence.

She pulled her gaze from his towel-wrapped body and bare legs and headed for the coffee pot. She hoped he didn't notice her hand shake as she poured a steamy mug for herself.

She sensed him, more than felt him come up behind her. He wrapped his arms around her and rested his head against hers.

She leaned against him, unable to pull away.

They stood, silently, as the kitchen clock ticked away on the wall behind them, each tick thunderously jarring across the quiet room. Harry sighed then finally released her and crossed back over to look out the window. She pressed the mug to her lips and the hot liquid warmed her lips. But it wasn't the warmth they craved. Her lips craved the warmth of another of Harry's kisses.

Harry watched as Sammy poured her coffee, then bustled around cleaning up the mess he'd made when he prepared the coffee. She carefully put the coffee, filters, and coffee scoop up in the cabinet, then crossed over to the trashcan to dump the grounds. She stopped and flipped on the radio on the counter. A peppy country song about living on a farm broke the silence in the room.

Sammy replaced the filter holder in the coffee maker with an efficient click. "I should go check on your clothes and see if they're dry yet."

Harry doubted they were, but he could tell Sammy wanted to escape. He nodded and she disappeared down the hallway.

A knock came from the front door, and he glanced down the hall, doubting Sammy heard it. He crossed over and opened the door.

A slightly familiar man stood in the doorway with a confused look on his face. His gaze slowly went from the wet hair on top of Harry's head down to his bare feet standing on the sandy carpet.

Too late, Harry realized he was dressed solely in a towel. His hand reached down to make sure the towel was tucked tightly at his waist.

The man was dressed smartly in business casual, right down to his expensive-looking leather loafers. Harry couldn't quite place where he'd seen him before.

The man stepped back. "I'm sorry. I must have the wrong address. I was looking for my daughter."

That was it.

Mr. Thompson.

"I... uh... no, come in. Sammy is here. She's just getting my clothes."

Well, that came out wrong.

"I mean... We got caught out in the storm. My clothes are drying in the dryer." Harry stepped aside to let Mr. Thompson enter, but not before the man gave him a I'm-not-sure-I-believe-that-story look.

"Dad." Sammy's voice came from behind him, sounding surprised. "What are you doing here?"

"I came to..." Mr. Thompson looked over at Harry again. "To check up on you. You're not answering my calls. I thought you might be in over your head." Mr. Thompson looked from Sammy to Harry. "In over your head on the Adriana Boutiques account, I mean."

"No, I'm fine. It's fine. But come in. Dad, this is

Harry. Harry, this is my father, I'm not sure if you remember him."

Mr. Thompson stared at Harry for a long moment, a frown crossing his face. "We've met before?"

"It was a long time ago."

"I'm afraid I don't remember."

"He was a, uh, friend of mine back when we used to come here every year."

"I see."

"We were out in the storm and got caught in the downpour. Harry's clothes are in the dryer."

"So he said." Mr. Thompson still didn't sound convinced.

Sammy rushed to change the subject. "We just made some coffee, do you want some?"

"Yes, that sounds good."

They all headed to the kitchen, Harry feeling woefully underdressed. Sammy poured her father a cup of coffee and motioned to the kitchen table. They all sat down.

None of them spoke. The radio crooned out a song about love gone wrong.

Mr. Thompson adjusted his chair, settling in for a long stay or possibly getting ready to bolt. He looked directly at Sammy. "So, do you have the Adriana account all wrapped up?"

"Just about." Sammy looked down at her coffee mug. "Well, I think so."

"So you haven't closed the deal?"

"I'm close. And I might have us another account. Hamilton Hotels."

"Really?" One of Mr. Thompson's eyebrows arched, impressed.

"I'm meeting with them again tomorrow afternoon."

Mr. Thompson put down his mug. "Let's meet tomorrow in the morning to review the presentation. I'll help you with it. Let's not let this chance pass us by. I should go now, though. It's getting late. I have a reservation at Belle Island Inn."

"No." Sammy's eyes grew wide. "I mean, you should stay here with me."

Sammy gave Harry a warning look. She obviously hadn't told her father that her mother was in town and staying at the inn.

"I don't want to put you out."

"Not at all, there's plenty of room." Sammy insisted, or pleaded, Harry couldn't tell which.

"Okay, I'll just cancel my reservation. I'll grab my suitcase and briefcase from the car." Mr. Thompson pushed away from the table and left the room. Harry could hear Sammy's father talking on his phone, cancelling the reservation.

"Harry, he doesn't know Mom is here." Sammy whispered.

"Don't you think you should tell him?" Harry eyed Sammy.

"I don't know how to tell him that. He's going to feel betrayed."

"It's a small town, Sams. He's bound to find out."

"Maybe I can hurry him into Sarasota, then get him to leave tomorrow."

"Maybe." Harry wasn't convinced it would turn out the way Sammy wanted it to. Secrets always had a way of coming out in the end.

CHAPTER 19

The next morning Sammy got up before dawn and quietly rushed around picking up the cottage. She was usually a neat person, but since being here on Belle Island, she'd gotten into the habit of just dropping things in her wake. A pair of shoes here, a colorful scarf there, a sweater tossed over the back of a chair. She snatched up her things and put them back in her bedroom.

She drove to The Sweet Shoppe and picked up some cinnamon rolls. She hurried back to the cottage and carefully, artfully, placed them on a serving tray. She brewed fresh coffee and the scent wafted around the kitchen. She took one last look around, making sure everything was in place before her father got up. She'd heard the water running from the direction of his bathroom, he was sure to be out any minute.

Her father walked into the kitchen looking every bit the professional business man. She looked down at her casual slacks and sweater. She'd planned on changing before they headed to Sarasota, but she felt self-consciously under dressed for the day so far.

She pasted on a smile. "Morning. Would you like some coffee? I picked up some breakfast from a shop here in town, too."

"That sounds great, thanks." Her father sat down at the kitchen table and placed his ever present worn leather notebook in front of him. He was ready to work. She recognized that look.

She poured coffee and placed the cinnamon rolls on some small, cheerful plates with starfish painted on the edges. She sat down and opened her own notebook. Time to work.

Her father seemed impressed with her work on the Adriana account. "I'm not sure why the deal isn't closed yet. It's an impressive campaign. Very original. I'm thinking the client's vision for her business isn't actually in alignment with her customers'. So she needs to change her vision, or be aware she needs to attract new clientele."

"Exactly. That's the problem. I'm not sure she wants to do either. I think she wants her current clients to accept her vision…"

"Well, we'll just have to see if we can sway her vision, won't we?" Her father jotted down some notes.

"Now, the Hamilton Hotels." He looked at her expectantly.

Sammy explained what her clients were hoping for and her promotional and advertising ideas. Her father nodded at some, wrinkled his forehead at some, but remained quiet until she'd finished.

"But I still think I'm missing something. I don't think it's exactly right. Not yet."

"Well, we'll just brainstorm some more ideas. I do think you're close. We just need a catchy tagline for them."

Her father was right. She needed a good phrase to add to the marketing campaign. "More coffee?"

Her father nodded. Sammy stood to go get the coffee pot. She turned when she heard a knock at the door. Must be Harry. She'd noticed he'd left his belt in the laundry room last night.

In spite of her best intentions, a smile spread across her face. She crossed to the door and swung it open.

"Good morning, Samantha. I brought some cinnamon rolls for your breakfast."

Her mother stood in the sunlight in frightening clarity. Sammy heard the kitchen chair scrape across the tile floor and clatter to the ground. Her father was standing behind her before she could manage to squeak out a word.

Her mother's eyes widened. "Phillip."

Her father moved close to her side, filling the doorway. He stood in silence, slowly taking in every inch of her mother, the exact same way Sammy had when she first saw her again. Sammy reached out and rested her hand on her father's arm.

Her father looked down at her hand without seeing it, and looked back at her mother. "Shelly. I didn't know you were here."

"I didn't know... I'm sorry. I didn't mean to interrupt. I didn't..." Her mother's words drifted off as she stood and stared at the man she'd been married to all those years ago.

The man she'd cheated on.

Her father cleared his throat. "You're in town to see Sammy, I guess? I didn't know you two were in contact with each other."

"We aren't. We *weren't*. I mean, I was here on the island and found out Sammy was here. I hadn't seen her since... in a very long time."

Her father turned and stared at Sammy. She shifted uneasily.

"Mom came by the cottage, then I went to talk to her for a bit yesterday. She's staying at the inn."

"So that's why you wanted me to cancel my reservation there."

"No. Well, kind of. I mean, I like having you stay here." Sammy looked from one parent to the other.

"I wanted so badly to see Samantha. To hear about her life now. See how she was doing. My parents show me photos and tell me the little they know about her now. I just... wanted to see her." Her mother's voice trailed off.

The three of them stood in awkward silence. Once a family, now a group of strangers.

"I have some calls to make. I'll make them in my bedroom and leave you two alone." Her father turned away and headed for the kitchen to grab his phone and notebook, but not before Sammy saw the hurt in his eyes.

After her father was safely tucked away in the back of the cottage, Sammy led her mother to the kitchen.

"Samantha, I'm so sorry. I shouldn't have just dropped by. I just thought after yesterday…"

"I know, Mom. It's okay. It's fine that you stopped by. I just hadn't found the right time to tell Dad you were here, too. He showed up last night. His visit was a surprise, too." Sammy poured her mom a mug of coffee and cleared off a space at the table. "Here, sit."

Sammy slipped into the chair next to her mom. "We must have been on the same wavelength today. I picked up cinnamon rolls, too."

"I got mine from this cute little bakery, The Sweet Shoppe." Her mother motioned to the box of pastry.

"Me, too." Sammy smiled.

"You always did have my sweet tooth." Her mother looked down at the box from The Sweet Shoppe.

Silence. Except for the ticking of the clock which Sammy had begun to realize was just too darn loud. She looked at her mother. The bangs on her forehead were swept to one side and a faded scar peaked through wisps of hair.

Her mother reached up self-consciously when she caught Sammy staring. "It's a scar from… from when I was in that accident with… Jonathan."

The accident where her lover was killed, but Sammy didn't say that.

"I still have a bit of a limp, especially when I'm tired. I had a broken hip and leg. Lots of surgery and rehab."

What did her mother want her to say, exactly? She wasn't comfortable talking about her mother and Jonathan. Sammy abruptly changed the subject. "Did you get caught out in that storm yesterday, too?"

Her mother paused, thrown off balance by the change in topics. "No, Dorothy knew someone and we went to their cottage and waited for the storm to pass. Then we got the call that they found Mary."

"I know. I was so glad to hear that."

Her mom sipped her coffee. "I met Mary last night after they got her back to the inn. And the adorable puppy she found, a darling Cavalier King Charles. She's calling him Stormy. She's going to look for his owners today, but in the meantime, I think the dog has stolen her heart."

Her mother set her mug on the table. "Did you get caught in the storm?"

"Yes, Harry and I were out looking by the bay. We ducked under the pier, but still got soaked."

"The young man was practically naked when I showed up." Her father entered the room. "Sorry, left my pen." He snatched up the pen from the table.

Her mother arched an eyebrow. "Naked?"

"No, Mom, he was drying his clothes. He had... um... a towel on." Sammy could feel the blush cross her cheeks. What was she? Sixteen again and justifying her actions to her parents? A rush of distant familiarity flooded over her. Just a normal family talk. Parents questioning their daughter.

But they weren't a family.

"He seemed like a nice enough young man. Poorly dressed, but nice enough." Her father didn't even crack a small smile like he usually did when he tossed out a wry remark.

"Dad!"

Her father ignored her unease and turned to her mother. "Are you planning on staying long, Shelly?"

Sammy couldn't tell from the tone of his voice if he was angry, uninterested, or making small talk.

"A few more days. I have some business to attend to."

"What kind of business?" Her father looked curiously at her mother.

"Something I should have dealt with long ago, but I didn't. I've been trying to clear things up from my past." Her mother turned her eyes to Sammy. "Make amends for choices I've made."

Her father gave his ex-wife a long, hard stare. With a brisk nod, he turned on his heels and walked to his room at the back of the cottage.

"He'll never forgive me." Her mother looked down at her hands, then back at Sammy. 'But, then, I'll never forgive myself."

CHAPTER 20

J ulie stood in front of the full-length mirror at Josephine's house. Susan and Tally sat with Josephine on the bed. The three women watched her as she turned this way and that.

"It didn't take Bella long to send these dresses down to try on." Josephine ran her hand over the lace on one of the dresses they'd unpacked. "Do you like that one you have on?"

Julie didn't want to hurt Josephine's feelings, but no, she didn't like it. Way too fussy. "I really appreciate Bella sending these dresses, but I'm not sure this one is the right one for me."

"Well, there's a note pinned to this next one. Bella says she thinks you'll like it best."

Julie crossed over to look at the dress Josephine had spread out on the bed. "I'll try it on next."

Julie went into the bathroom to slip on yet another dress. She'd lost count of how many dresses she'd tried on in this tortuous hunt for the perfect wedding gown. She wished she could get more excited about the whole wedding thing, she did. But… it all seemed so overwhelming, from dresses to guests, invitations to flowers, and everything else in between.

Julie could hear the women chatting as she slipped into Bella's favorite. She went out into the bedroom again. "Can someone do up the buttons? At least some of them? I think there might be two hundred buttons down the back of this."

Tally jumped up, hurried over, and started on the buttons. "You're right. There might be hundreds on here. I'll just do up some of them until we see how it fits."

Julie stood in front of the mirror again. Much to her surprise, she liked this dress. A bit old-fashioned, with a satiny skirt covered in simple lace with delicate long sleeves.

"Bella says this one is probably from the early fifties. It's called a ballerina length."

Julie spun around slowly. "I like it. It's different and doesn't look anything like bridal gowns do now.

It feels like it's connected with history and permanence." She blushed. "I'm sounding a bit crazy now, aren't I?"

"Not at all." Susan came to stand beside her. "There is something comforting about connecting with the past. And you look beautiful in it."

"Do you think Reed will like it? I want to look like his version of a real bride."

"I do."

Julie hated to admit to herself that she might finally get into the whole wedding thing, if only she could decide on a dress. This dress was like the bridal gowns she'd dreamed of when she was a little girl. A real wedding gown, but different.

She smoothed the skirt and something rustled beneath her hand. She pulled up the lace and found a small pocket sewn into the satin layer of the dress. She slipped her hand into the pocket and pulled out a crinkled piece of paper.

"What's that?" Tally peered over her shoulder.

Julie carefully unfolded the paper and read the words out loud.

~

I don't know who will end up with this wedding dress of mine. I was married to the love of my life in

December 1950. We were married for sixty-two years before he passed away. I'm moving to a nursing home now and must part with my beloved dress. I hope it finds just the right person and I pray that whoever ends up with this dress finds as much happiness as I did.

I wish you a beautiful wedding and years of love.

~

With much love and blessings for your life together,

~

Barbara

~

The four women remained silent while Julie fought off tears. Susan wrapped her in a hug, her arms comforting and familiar.

Julie cleared her throat. "I'm certain this dress was meant for me. It's perfect. I'll cherish it always."

Julie sucked in a long breath and turned to look in the mirror again. And just like that, the wedding dress dilemma was solved.

~

Julie went to Reed's beach house, well *her* beach house now, *their* beach house. It still took some getting used to for her to think of it that way. She couldn't wait to let him know she'd found a wedding dress. She was almost certain he thought she was just stalling picking a dress so she could postpone the wedding. After all, it had taken her forever to even set a date for their nuptials.

"Reed?" She called out as she entered the house.

"Out on the deck." Reed's voice filtered through the open French door.

He turned when she came outside and held out his arms. She smiled and crossed the distance. He hugged her close as she leaned against him.

"To what do I owe this midday surprise?"

"I found a wedding dress!"

"You did?" He looked skeptical. "Where is it?"

"Susan took it home. She's going to iron it all up for me. Besides, I don't want you to see it before the wedding."

"So, you're getting all superstitious and old-fashioned about the wedding now?" He cocked his head to one side.

Julie laughed. "Funny you should say that."

Reed looked totally confused and Julie laughed again. "Never mind, but the dress is perfect."

"I have to admit I like seeing you get excited

about the wedding. Not too long ago I wasn't sure I'd even be able to get you to walk down the aisle."

"I'm getting used to this whole wedding idea. Susan and Tally are helping me. We don't need gifts, so there is no registering or anything like that." Julie frowned. "The people you're inviting will be okay with that, right?"

Reed shrugged. "They'll have to be. It's what my wife-to-be wants. And, honestly, we don't need anything. Well, except I need you." Reed winked at her.

She tossed back her head and laughed again. Reed made her happy. She was bubbling with happiness these days. Her life was turning into something she'd never imagined she'd have for herself. She and Reed would be a family.

"So you going to tell me anything about the dress?"

Julie grinned at him. "I sure will. It's white."

He chuckled and leaned down to kiss her. "That's for giving me *all* those details."

"I just want to make sure you know which one is the bride when it comes to our wedding day," she teased.

"Woman, I'd know you even if I were blindfolded and waiting at the end of the aisle for you."

CHAPTER 21

After a meeting with the Adriana account that afternoon, Sammy could see why her father was so successful at his business. He had the owner charmed and agreeing to the new campaign within fifteen minutes. They closed the deal and although Sammy would have liked to have secured the account herself, she was grateful for her father's expertise and glad that she hadn't lost the account to another firm.

They headed back to Belle Island and decided to grab dinner at Magic Cafe. Her father pulled into a parking spot in the crushed shell lot, and they walked to the front door of the restaurant, the shells crunching beneath their steps.

Tally was there to greet them. "Sammy, good to see you."

"Tally, I don't know if you remember him, but this is my father."

"Ah, Mr. Thompson, good to see you."

"Call me Phillip, please."

"Phillip it is." Tally grabbed some menus from the hostess station. "Inside or out?"

"Out please. Oh, Dad, is that okay?"

"Fine by me."

Tally set them up at a table by the edge of the beach. "Can I get you some drinks? Here's our drink list. We have a nice selection of wine, not extensive, but good wines."

Her father reached for the menu. "Let me look at it for a minute."

"Sounds good, I'll send your waitress over."

Sammy watched her Dad scan the list and nod approvingly. "Would you like a red wine tonight? They have a nice cabernet."

"That sounds fine."

"Or let's look at the menu first, then decide." They looked at their menus, trying to decide what to order. Sammy was leaning toward the grouper yet again.

She looked up and saw her mother entering the restaurant from the beach, her hair blowing in the breeze, her cheeks red from the wind. She clutched a bright wrap around her shoulders. Their eyes met and her mother paused. Sammy looked from her mother to her father.

She reached out and touched her father's arm. "Dad, Mom's here. She just walked in. I swear I didn't tell her we were coming here or anything."

"I see." Her father set his menu on the table. "Well, go invite her to join us."

Sammy looked from one parent to the other. "Really?"

"Of course. It's ridiculous for her to sit at another table like she doesn't even know us. She's your mother."

Sammy jumped up and hurried over to her mom. "Dad said I should ask you to join us."

Her mother's eyes widened. "Are you sure?"

"Yes, of course, come join us." Sammy hoped her voice sounded as confident as the words she said.

She led the way back to their table and her father stood and held out a chair for her mother. Her mom slipped gracefully onto the seat without missing a beat. How had this happened, the three of them eating together after all these years?

Sammy sank onto her chair and took a deep breath. This was going to be an interesting meal...

"There's a good cab on the wine list, would you like some?" Her father sat down as if the three of them sharing a meal was an everyday occurrence. "Or, if you still enjoy sparkling, there is a nice sparkling rose."

"I do still like sparkling."

"I do, too. That sounds good to me, Dad." Sammy shifted in her chair, watching her parents.

Tally came over with another menu. "I see you've added to your table."

"Tally, you remember my mother?"

"I do. It's very nice to see you." Tally smiled like nothing strange was going on. "Have you decided on drinks?"

"Your sparkling rose, please." Her father handed the wine list back to Tally. "You do have a nice wine list."

"Thank you. Nothing like a nice glass of wine with a good meal."

Tally went off to fetch their wine and Sammy pretended to study the menu. Not that she needed to, she'd decided on the grouper. It was safe. It was a decision she really didn't have to think about. She needed something safe and familiar while the evening spun out of control.

She watched her parents from the corner of her eye. Her mother was looking at her menu as intently as Sammy. Her father was looking around the restaurant and taking in the view of the ocean, oddly calm.

The waitress delivered their wine and her father poured a glass for each of them. To Sammy's surprise, he raised his glass. "To Belle Island, may she never change."

The three of them clinked glasses. Her father's fingers grazed her mom's hand. Her mother slowly pulled her drink to her lips and took a small sip. Sammy was pretty sure the evening couldn't get any stranger.

And then it did.

Harry stood at the opening to Magic Cafe, craving some of Tally's seafood and a good, cold beer. He'd wanted to ask Sammy to come with him, but knew her father was staying with her. After her father had caught him there in just a towel, he wasn't sure he wanted to face the man again. He looked around the restaurant and froze when he saw Sammy.

And her mother.

And her father.

At the same table.

Sammy waved to him with an obvious, come-on-over motion.

He wove his way over to the table, not sure what he was walking into. The last he'd heard their family was irreparably split, yet there they were, having a meal together.

"Harry, you should join us." Sammy's eyes held the tiniest bit of pleading.

"Nice to see you more appropriately dressed," Sammy's father said dryly.

"Um, yes." Harry stood by the table, thinking maybe he should have stayed home tonight and cooked.

"Harry, you remember my mother."

Harry looked at the woman at the table. Impeccably dressed in a casual way. Looking younger than he knew she had to be. He smiled at her and held out his hand. "Yes, nice to see you again, Mrs. —" *What was her name now?*

The woman reached for his hand and gave him a warm smile in return. "It's good to see you again, too. Please, just call me Shelly."

Sammy's father watched Harry carefully then leaned back in his chair, his arms crossed over his chest.

"You'll join us?" There was that hint of begging in Sammy's voice now.

Harry looked at her father, waiting for some sign from him.

"Yes, of course, join us." The words were welcoming, but the tone, not so much.

Sammy grabbed his hand and tugged him into the chair beside her. "We haven't ordered yet." She waved for the waitress. "I bet you want a beer."

A beer or two...

Harry ordered an Abita beer and took a long, thankful swig as soon as it arrived.

"So Harry, what do you do?" Sammy's father asked a friendly enough question but with an undertone of interrogation.

"I own Island Property Management here in town."

"Oh. Been doing that long?"

"Quite a few years."

"Do you like living on the island?" Shelly smiled when she asked the question. "I think it would be a lovely place to live. I always did love the island."

Sammy's father stared at her mother. Shelly took another sip of wine, oblivious to Mr. Thompson's gaze.

Harry took another quick swallow of beer. "I... uh... I do like it here. I have friends, the weather is usually great, except when it isn't." He grinned.

"The business is growing. Yes, I'm happy here." Harry realized he *was* happy here, not that he thought about it often. Though he wondered if he would still be as happy here after Sammy left…

"Where do you live?" Her father grilled him again.

"I have an apartment over Island Property Management on Oak Street, but I spend a lot of time in different properties fixing them up for the owners. I'm actually living in Bellemire right now."

That awkward silence settled over the table. Sammy set down her glass and shot him a look. But what kind of look? He wasn't sure. Heck, he wasn't sure about anything right now except he was *positive* he should have stayed home and cooked his dinner.

Shelly leaned forward on the table. "You're living in Bellemire now?"

"I'm fixing it up for… a friend."

"Bellemire Cottage is why I'm in town."

"It is?" Harry frowned.

"Yes. It appears there was some confusion on the deed when it was sold. I'm here trying to clear it up. I want to get the cottage back for my parents."

"You can't." Harry and Sammy said the words in perfect unison.

He looked at Sammy, then her mother.

"Why not? I do have legal right to it. I've been

working with a real estate lawyer. I want to pay back my parents for all…" Shelly looked down at her hands, then looked up at Sammy's father. "They lost a lot trying to help me. They paid for my mistakes. All of you did."

Mr. Thompson sat silently with no sign that he acknowledged he'd even heard what his ex-wife said.

"Mom, you can't. I mean, I actually wanted to buy it back for Grams and Pops, but it can't happen now. It won't work."

"You were going to buy it?" Her mother frowned.

"I was, but you see, it's owned by a trust now and… well, Harry is fixing it up for Rose."

Shelly's forehead wrinkled and her eyes clouded with confusion. Sammy looked at him as if asking for his permission. He nodded.

"See, Rose—she's a friend of Harry's—she's in a wheelchair. Harry has converted the cottage to be wheelchair accessible for Rose. She graduates from college this spring and will move into the cottage. It just didn't seem right to try and take it away, not when it had already been converted."

Shelly sat back in her chair, a perplexed look on her face. "That does complicate things."

"So you see, Mom, that's why you can't try to get the cottage now."

"My lawyer has already started the proceedings."

"Can't you stop them?"

"I don't know. I'm afraid it's going to bring up the legitimacy of the current deed no matter what I do."

Harry let out a long breath. All he wanted was to give Rose a nice place to live on the beach. Why did it have to be so complicated?

Her mother looked at Harry. "I'm sorry, Harry. I had no idea about all of this."

Sammy sighed. The night couldn't get much crazier at this point, could it?

"It's okay. I hope we can get it all straightened out, though. Rose really deserves the cottage. She... well, she's a great person."

"Maybe we should all order. We can't solve the legal problems tonight." Her father picked up his menu. Sammy didn't miss that he'd ignored her mother's comment about making a mistake all those years ago.

They all ordered and then proceeded to have awkward small talk. Sammy figured after they depleted chatting about the weather in each season on Belle Island and how the town had changed, or not changed, that there was nothing else to talk about. They finished their meal in silence.

After the meal, her father paid the tab, even though Harry offered to pay. "If you'll excuse me for a moment." Her father got up and walked inside.

Her mother sat quietly sipping the last of the decaf coffee she'd ordered.

"You okay, Mom?"

Her mother smiled. "I'm fine. It was just a strange evening, wasn't it?"

"I'll say," Sammy answered with a bit too much gusto.

"I didn't think we'd all three ever be sitting at the same table again."

"I wasn't even sure I'd ever see you again." Sammy reached out and touched her mother's hand. "I'm glad you came to the island, and I'm glad I was here."

"Me too, sweetie."

Her father returned to the table. "I've called the inn and they have a room for me. I appreciate the offer of staying with you, Samantha, but I think I'll move to the inn." He turned to her mother. "If that's not too awkward for you?"

"No, not at all."

"That way, Samantha can do what she needs to

do. I'll stay a few days and work from my room and see if Samantha needs any help before I leave."

"Dad, you're welcome at the cottage."

"Thanks, but I'll let you enjoy your cottage, and your time at the beach. I'll move to the inn."

Sammy looked from her father to her mother. Her mother was glancing, surreptitiously, at her father over the top of her coffee mug.

Okay, maybe the night could get crazier.

CHAPTER 22

Sammy's father took her back to the cottage, and in spite of her protests, packed his bags. He came out from the back room, his suitcase in one hand and computer bag in the other.

"Dad, you don't have to leave."

"I know. But I'll let you get on with your presentation to Hamilton Hotels without interfering. Though, you know I'm here if you need help or want me to come to your meeting."

"I've got it, Dad. I'm pretty sure I'll have it wrapped up this week."

"I got a small suite at the inn with a sitting area and desk. I'll work from there for a few days. I might even poke around the island a bit."

"What? You're taking some time off? Say it isn't

KAY CORRELL

so." Sammy teased her father. She couldn't remember the last time he'd taken so much as a day off work.

"The weather is supposed to be unseasonably warm the next few days. Wouldn't mind a few walks on the beach. Might even go out to the lighthouse."

Somehow Sammy doubted if her father would make a wish and toss a shell into the ocean.

Her father set his suitcase and computer on the floor. "Tonight was... not what I'd expected."

"Me neither. I just... it was strange and familiar at the same time, you know?" Sammy didn't know how she felt about the evening. She needed time to sit and think, process her thoughts. "I was glad you said to ask Mom to join us though."

Her father crossed over and looked out the window at the stars blinking in the inky darkness of the night sky. "At first I just said to invite her because it would have been so awkward for her to be sitting at the same restaurant at a different table." He traced a finger along the weathered window frame. "I've spent so long being angry at your mother. Furious at what she did. Blaming her for breaking up the family."

"I'm sorry she hurt you, Dad."

"She did. I *was* very hurt. I lashed out and prevented her from seeing you, which was wrong.

202

She was still your mother. I just wanted to hurt her back, like she'd hurt me. I'm sorry about that now." He turned to her. "I wish things had been different, but we can't change the past."

"I was mad at her, too. I didn't want to see her back then. But when she came here this week… I couldn't bear to *not* see her, to not talk to her."

"I've spent a lot of years blaming your mother, but if I'm really honest with myself, I was never there for her. I was all about business all the time. I know she needed more from me. She *told* me she needed more. That she didn't need all the things I bought her, she just wanted more time with me. She once told me that she'd never been lonelier than being married to me." A look of regret and pain flashed across her father's face. "I should have listened to her. Really listened. But I didn't."

Her father sighed. "I'm not saying having an affair was the right thing to do, it wasn't. But, after all these years, I can begin to understand why she just wanted someone to appreciate her. I never told her thank you for all she did for me, for how she made my life easier. Honestly, I probably didn't even tell her I loved her after the first few years of our marriage. I'm as much responsible for our family falling apart as she was. Her action was just the final blow."

Sammy perched on the edge of the sofa, trying not to let her mouth gape open. "Dad, I don't even know what to say."

"There isn't much to say, is there?"

"I know Mom was lonely in Chicago. I know she loved to come to Belle Island and be with her parents and have people around all the time." Sammy picked up a pillow from the sofa and hugged it to her chest. "That night. If only I hadn't accused Mom in front of everyone. I should have handled it differently. Talked to her. I ruined everything for our family."

Her father crossed over and set his hand on her shoulder. "None of this is your fault. Your mother and I are to blame, each in different ways. I took her for granted. Took our family for granted. Your mother's greatest sin was just wanting to be loved and appreciated." Her father tilted her chin up so she would look directly at him. "But none of this, *none*, is your fault."

Her father turned away, gathered his things and walked out of the cottage.

Sammy remained perched on the arm of the sofa, lost in thought.

Harry had waited until he saw Sammy's father leave and slipped around to the ocean side of the cottage. The sand sunk beneath his feet as he rounded the corner of the house. He climbed the steps up the deck. He could see Sammy through the French door, sitting on the arm of the sofa.

The woman did love to perch on things.

Determined, he took quick steps across the deck and rapped on the door. Sammy looked up in surprise, then motioned for him to come in.

He opened the door, spilling cool sea air into the room. The wind blew some papers off the table by the door and he bent over to pick them up. He closed the door behind him and placed the papers back on the table, unsure what to say or do. He'd just known he needed to come see Sammy.

He finally crossed over and sat on the sofa. Sammy slid down next to him.

"It was quite a night, wasn't it?" He ignored the fact she was inches away from him.

"You have no idea." Sammy shoved her hair back from her face. "My dad… he… oh, I don't even know how to explain. He said that he thinks he's as much to blame for our family falling apart as my mom is. That he never had time for her. He took her for granted. He knew she was lonely and did nothing to change things."

Sammy looked up at him, her brown eyes glistening with tears. "It's like my whole life is tilting off axis. Everything that I knew as the truth is shifting. He said that it isn't my fault the family fell apart. None of it. He doesn't blame me for confronting Mom in front of everyone all those years ago."

"Wow, that's a lot to process." He couldn't help himself. He slowly reached out and wiped a lone tear that tracked down Sammy's cheek. He wanted to help her, make her feel better, take away her pain.

"I feel like I'm standing on quicksand. Hoping that maybe my family can have some kind of civil relationship now, but afraid to believe it. That maybe it will be okay with my dad if I get to know my mother again."

"I think it would be good for you to get reacquainted with your mom."

Sammy nodded. "I want to. I do. If it doesn't hurt Dad. Everything is so confusing right now."

He reached over and wiped another tear away, then left his hand on her cheek. She reached up to cover his hand and pressed it against her. He couldn't help himself. He leaned down and kissed her slowly and gently.

She kissed him back, then reached her arms to

encircle his neck. He pulled her close and kissed her again.

She sighed.

He kissed her yet again, his heart hammering in his chest. He was standing on that same quicksand Sammy was, hoping yet afraid to believe. Hoping for one last chance with Sammy. Hoping he wouldn't screw it up.

She pulled back and looked him directly in the eyes. "I'm not sure that kiss makes things less confusing for me, Harry."

CHAPTER 23

The next morning Harry looked up from his desk at Island Property Management to see Camille standing in his doorway. He stood. "Camille, come in. What can I do for you?" Camille and her mother had rented some large beach properties from him near their own beach home when they'd had some large parties. He figured it was about time for another one of their huge, fancy bashes.

"Harry..." Camille shifted nervously from foot to foot.

"Here, take a seat." Harry motioned to a chair by his desk.

Camille gracefully slid into the seat and placed

her purse on her lap, fiddling with the shoulder strap. "My mother wanted me to come talk to you."

"Do you need me to look into some more rentals for you? Having another party?"

"No, it's not that. Harry, we're thinking of renting out *our* beach house."

Harry hoped he'd quickly wiped off the stunned expression he knew had flooded his face. "Oh?" Harry couldn't imagine the Montgomerys wanting strangers in their home.

Camille looked down at her purse, then at Harry. "Well, we're just not interested in coming here very often anymore. I think Momma has grown tired of the island."

"Really?"

"Well, there is really no good way to get here. The drive is getting too long for her, and flying entails driving to New Orleans and then flying to Tampa for a direct flight, or Sarasota is closer, but there are no direct flights. It's just tedious."

"I see. Well, I'd be glad to handle the rental for you."

"Momma asked me to clear out some of our good things. I'm having them shipped to her home in Comfort Crossing. But we're hoping you can get it on the rental market as soon as possible."

"I can do that. Do you want me to give you a copy of our rental agreement?"

"Oh, I don't want to see it. Just send it to our lawyer." Camille dug in her purse, brought out a business card, and handed it to Harry. "Here's his card. He'll take care of all the details and make sure you're listing it at a fair rental price."

Harry pasted on a smile. He knew his business. He knew what he could get for the rental. Hopefully the lawyer wouldn't give him much trouble.

Camille stood. "Thank you. I hope you can get this done immediately. I'll have the things we want cleared out by the end of the week."

"I'll send the contract to your lawyer today."

"Perfect." Camille flipped her hair behind her shoulder.

He couldn't miss a fleeting sadness slip across her face before she turned to leave. She glided to the door—how did some women manage to glide when they walked?

She turned to him. "Thank you, Harry." Camille's voice was low and he'd swear she was near tears. She cleared her throat and disappeared without another word.

Well, that was strange.

~

Harry slipped into The Lucky Duck for a quick lunch with Jamie. Harry took a seat at the bar and Willie came over.

"Hey, Harry. Good to see you. Meeting Jamie?"

"I am. I'm a bit early though."

"Can I get you anything while you wait?" Willie plopped down a bowl of nuts in front of him.

"Iced tea."

"I'll have the same." Jamie walked up behind him, then slid onto the barstool beside him.

"Two teas, coming up."

"How's your day going?" Jamie asked as he grabbed a few nuts from the bowl on the bar.

"Strange."

"How so?" Jamie cocked his head to the side.

"So, Camille Montgomery came in. They want me to handle renting out their beach house. I never thought I'd see the day the Montgomerys would want anyone to use their house."

Jamie frowned.

"Why are you giving me that look?" Harry looked closely at his friend.

"I… well, I shouldn't say anything. But, well, since you're doing business with them, I'm going to give you a heads up. I think the Montgomerys might be having financial problems."

"No kidding?"

"Just a few things that have happened. Cindy has picked up on some of it. Not spreading gossip, but I do think they might be going through a rough patch."

"Well, that would make sense. Maybe that's why they are renting out the house. Bring in some income. It should do pretty well, it's a nice property."

Willie came over. "Didn't mean to overhear what you said, but... there is some talk around town about the Montgomerys. I do think they are having problems. They evidently have a large, unpaid bill with the pool maintenance company and one with that fancy decorator store in Sarasota for some furniture they ordered."

"How do you always know what's going on in town?" Harry looked at Willie.

Willie grinned. "People come and sit at the bar and talk. Everyone opens up to the bartender. It's like a life rule or something."

Harry laughed. "I guess it is. Anyway, thanks for the heads up. And I'll have to make sure the pool is taken care of if they're going to rent it."

Willie walked off to help some other customers.

"It's kind of unfathomable to think about the Montgomerys hitting hard times, isn't it? They've always been *that family*. The ones with everything and throwing lavish parties." Jamie shook his head. "And, Camille has always let everyone know she's all that. She's treated Cindy badly at the Hamilton."

"Camille is kind of her own worst enemy, isn't she?" Harry agreed.

"Well, it looks like she might have some real changes coming." Jamie shook his head. "Anyway, I hear that Sammy is presenting her promotional plan for the Hamilton Hotels tomorrow. Hope it goes well. I know that both Cindy and Adam think highly of her."

"I hope it goes well for her, too." Though, Harry wasn't quite ready for Sammy to get the account, because then she'd be headed back to Chicago, which was not what he wanted.

"Maybe they should push the meeting back a few days, give her more time to prepare." Harry took a sip of his drink.

Jamie laughed. "You mean give her a few more days here with you."

Harry sighed. "You know me so well."

~

Cindy crossed through the lobby after finishing up with the meeting regarding the promotional plans for the Hamilton Hotel and the new Beverly Hamilton. She'd been impressed with Samantha's presentation and knew the woman was on the right track. She'd left the meeting before Adam and Mr. Hamilton had made their final decision, but she hoped they'd give the account to Samantha.

She had another meeting in five minutes that she didn't want to miss. She pulled out her cell phone and checked her text messages. She read a strange one from Jamie about Camille Montgomery putting her family's beach house up for rent. That seemed unusual. She slipped the phone back into her pocket.

Her text message must have messed with the universe, because Cindy looked up and Camille was entering The Hamilton. Cindy looked around to see if she could duck away without being seen. She wasn't really up for any of Camille's pointed remarks today.

Too late.

Camille walked directly towards her with quick, definite steps. "Cindy. I'm looking for Delbert."

"He's in a meeting right now. He should be finished fairly soon."

"But I need to speak to him now."

Cindy wasn't sure how to answer that one. It wasn't her job to run interference for Mr. Hamilton. "I'm sure he'll be out soon."

"I…" Camille paused.

Cindy looked closely at the woman and she'd swear Camille had been crying. Her eyes were puffy and her usually perfectly done makeup was… not so perfect. "Are you okay?" Cindy couldn't keep herself from asking.

"Of course." Camille looked down. "Well, no. I'm not. I… well, I've had some difficult news this week. It's been a bad day. I just…" Camille sighed. "I just wanted to talk to Delbert. He always knows the right thing to say to me."

Cindy tried to keep the astonished look off her face. She couldn't believe Camille was having a civil conversation with her, much less opening up. "I'm sorry you're having a rough time."

Camille nodded.

"You could come wait in my office until Mr. Hamilton is ready."

Camille looked relieved. "Thank you. That would be nice."

Cindy led the way to her office, cleared files off of one of the chairs, and Camille took a seat.

"Can I get you anything? Coffee or tea?"

"No, I'm fine." Camille's voice didn't sound like she was fine.

Cindy looked at the clock on her desk. If she didn't leave right now, she was going to be late for her meeting. With a quick look at Camille, she picked up her phone. "Nancy, will you call Mr. Belleview and tell him I'll be late. If he wants to reschedule, that's fine. Just put it on my calendar."

Camille looked up. "You don't need to cancel because of me. I don't want to keep you."

"No, it's fine." Cindy leaned against the desk.

"I don't know why you're being so kind to me. I'm usually... kind of short with you."

Cindy kept her mouth from falling open, but just barely. Short with her, that was one way to put it. "I..." She cleared her throat. "I can tell you're having a bad day." She didn't mention the text from Jamie.

"I... well, I have a hard time with... people. I always seem to say the wrong thing. Oh, I can do great in social situations, at parties, and things like that. But... I don't really have any close friends. Sometimes I'm surprised Delbert is still dating me."

Cindy was at a loss on what to say.

"I don't know why I'm telling you all this." Camille opened her purse, took out a tissue, and dabbed at her eyes.

"I'm a good listener."

A tiny smile graced Camille's face. "You are. I appreciate that." Camille took a small mirror out of her purse and glanced at her reflection. "Oh, goodness, I'm a mess. I should go fix my face before Delbert sees me like this."

"Like what?" Mr. Hamilton's voice came from the open doorway. "I thought I heard your voice in here."

"Oh, Delbert." Camille jumped up and hurried over to Mr. Hamilton.

He put a hand on each of her shoulders and looked closely at her. "What's wrong?"

"I should have listened to you. You were right. Everything is so… horrible." Camille's shoulders trembled.

"Don't cry, honey." Mr. Hamilton gave Camille a quick hug. "Come with me. We'll go find a quiet place to talk."

Camille nodded and started to follow Mr. Hamilton from the room. She paused and turned back. "Cindy, thank you for… well, for listening to me. You've been very kind."

Cindy finally allowed her mouth to gape open as the couple walked out of her office.

CHAPTER 24

Sammy grinned on the drive back from Sarasota. She'd gotten the Hamilton Hotel deal. *She'd gotten the deal!* All on her own. She'd hardly been able to keep herself from spinning around crazily in the lobby on her way out. Instead she'd sung along with the radio, at the top of her lungs, all the way back to Belle Island.

She couldn't wait to tell her father. She'd started to call and tell him, but decided she wanted to tell him in person. This was her first big account she'd closed all on her own. She was pretty darn proud of herself.

She pulled into the parking lot at Belle Island Inn. The early afternoon sun was exceptionally warm for this time of year and soaked through to her very bones. She better enjoy this, since Chicago was still getting hammered with cold, snowy winter weather. She quickly refused to consider the next thought that popped into her mind. She purposely ignored the fact that when she left, she'd no longer get to see Harry every day. She had no idea when she'd even see him again after she returned home.

But she wasn't going to think about that. She wasn't.

With determined strides, she crossed over to the inn and pushed inside. Dorothy was at the reception desk and greeted her with a welcoming smile. "Sammy, good to see you."

"Hi, Dorothy. How's Mary doing today?"

"She's just fine. All recovered from her big adventure the other day. She's been taking Stormy for walks on the beach. The puppy is the cutest thing I've ever seen. Mary is besotted with him." Dorothy grinned. "Anyway, we all sure appreciate your help looking for her."

"Glad to help. I'm just happy she was found safe."

Dorothy nodded.

"I'm looking for my father. Do you know him?"

"I do. I saw him head into the restaurant a while ago for a late lunch."

"Thanks, Dorothy."

Sammy headed to the inn's restaurant, anxious to tell her dad the good news. She stood in the entranceway and scanned the room. "Oh," she gasped and took a step back. There in her line of view was her father.

Having lunch.

With her *mother*.

She took another quick step back and whirled away from the entrance. Now was not the time to talk to her father.

She hurried across the lobby and burst out into the bright sunshine. Her mother and father were having lunch. *Together*.

The world as she knew it, had known it for twenty years, was disintegrating right before her eyes. But was that such a bad thing?

"Sams." Harry called out to her a second time. She'd come rushing out of the inn with the most bewildered look on her face. He jogged up to her. "Sammy, you okay?"

She finally looked up at him, a confused look in her eyes. "Oh. Hi, Harry. What are you doing here?"

"Jamie wants me to look at one of the stoves. They're having problems with the pilot light."

"Oh." Sammy's voice held no interest in his reply. It was like she barely heard him.

"Are you okay?" He repeated his question.

She looked up at him. "I think so. I just—you won't believe this—I just saw my parents having lunch together at the inn."

"Well, that's surprising."

"I know." Sammy's eyes glazed with a dazed look. "I just got out of there as quickly as I could. I didn't want to interrupt."

"So... what do you think is up with that?"

"Honestly, I have no clue. I mean we accidentally all had dinner last night at Magic Cafe, but... I don't know what to make of this."

"It would be nice if you all could have some kind of relationship again." Harry looked for Sammy's reaction.

"It would. Wouldn't it? I mean..." Sammy hesitated. "These last few weeks have been so confusing."

"But they've also been pretty darn nice, Sams. At least for me."

She looked at him, but he couldn't read her expression. He quickly changed the subject, knowing this wasn't a good time to discuss their relationship. "So, Jamie said you were meeting with Adam about the Hamilton account. How did that go?"

Sammy's eyes sparkled with delight. "I got the account." She swirled around once, laughing out loud.

"That's great."

Sammy was grinning now. "I was coming over here to tell my dad."

"I'm sure they wouldn't mind if you went in there and told them."

"Probably, but Harry..." She looked up at him. "I just didn't want to bother them while they are... together."

CHAPTER 25

Harry sat at his desk at Island Property Management late that afternoon. He'd fixed the pilot light for Jamie and because he couldn't help himself, he'd peeked into the dining room before he'd left to see Sammy's parents sitting together an hour later. He wasn't sure what to make of it.

He realized he'd been sitting staring at his desk for almost thirty minutes and he'd done nothing. His mind was filled with thoughts. How long it would take to finish up Bellemire Cottage, if Sammy's family would find a way to be a family again—and most importantly, how much longer Sammy would be here.

He wanted to ask her to stay on the island, but

how fair would that be to her? She had her job back in Chicago. She'd never leave her father's company, that much she'd made perfectly clear to him. And he couldn't ask her to. His job was here on the island. He knew beach property rentals and maintenance, he knew nothing about city buildings, property rentals, and city regulations in a town like Chicago. He was considered a successful businessman on Belle Island, and he admitted he liked that. He'd worked hard for that. Plus, he wanted to be around for Rose. He owed her that.

If only things had been different long ago, maybe their lives wouldn't have traveled in two different directions, so very, very far apart.

His heart rested heavily in his chest. After the last few weeks, he couldn't imagine what life would be like around here without Sammy.

Sammy got up from the table at the cottage to answer the knock at the door. Her father stood in the doorway. "I thought I'd drop by and see how your presentation to Hamilton Hotels went today."

Her father looked… relaxed. She narrowed her eyes and stared at him, puzzled. When was the last time she'd seen him look relaxed?

"Samantha?"

"Oh, sorry, Dad. Come in." She stood aside to let him in and led him over to the sofa by the window.

Her dad sat and looked at her expectantly.

"I got it." Sammy grinned, wanting to whirl around the room, but needing to project a proper successful businesswoman image.

Her father smiled. "I never doubted you would. I'm very proud of you, honey."

"Thanks, Dad. I'm pretty proud of myself, too." Sammy balanced on the arm of the sofa.

"I should take you out to celebrate tonight." Her father looked at his watch.

All Sammy could think of was that he couldn't possibly be hungry yet, he'd just finished a late lunch with her mother…

"I, uh. I have plans already. Harry asked me to dinner."

"Oh, well, I wouldn't want to interfere with your plans."

"You could join us," Sammy offered.

"No, but thanks. You go have fun." Her father looked around the cottage. "It's kind of nice being back down here on Belle Island, isn't it?"

Now, that was one of the last things she thought she'd hear come out of her father's mouth.

"It is. I'd forgotten how much I've missed it."

"It's a shame your mother couldn't get Bellemire back for her parents. They might have enjoyed that. She told me she settled the legal matters regarding the deed. Your friend, Harry, is good to go. No problems with the title anymore."

"That's great. He'll be so relieved."

"So, Dad. *You* owned the cottage back then?"

Her father looked at her. "I did."

"I always thought Grams and Pops owned it."

"They were going to buy it, but you know how Pops is, he was afraid to tie up their retirement in real estate. So I bought it for them. The only way they'd accept was to pay me fair rental value on it."

"I didn't know."

"Anyway, after…" Her father paused and looked out the window. "After Shelly's accident, they could no longer afford to keep paying the rent. They needed to help pay Shelly's medical bills. I told them they didn't have to pay rent, I was okay with that. But, your Pops wouldn't hear of it. They moved to that small apartment in Orlando in that retirement community."

"I had no idea."

"I sold the place because… well, it just held bad memories and no one in the family used it. Since I still owned it when your mother and I got divorced, she still had rights to it when I sold it. She was in the hospital by then, and the paperwork got messed up because your Pops was power of attorney for your mother for a bit while she was in rehab."

"So that's how it all happened."

"Your mother signed a quit claim deed to the cottage now, and I just transferred her half the proceeds from the sale. It was the right thing to do."

So they'd just been talking about all this legal stuff at lunch. Sammy's heart squeezed as disappointment flooded through her. She'd been foolish to think that maybe they could be some kind of family again.

Her father stood. "I should go and let you get ready for dinner. I'm really proud of you, I want you to know that."

Sammy got up from her perch on the sofa arm. "Thanks, Dad."

He turned as he walked to the door. "You headed back to Chicago now? I have a flight out in the morning. I could book you a seat on it."

"I… sure, that would be great."

Her father left and she went to stand by the window, staring out at the ocean. That was great, right? She could get back to Chicago and her apartment. Water her plants, go through her mail, get back to real life.

Her real life that she was fairly confident would be full of lonely, gloomy days.

Sammy sat on the swing with Harry later that night after walking back from their dinner at Magic Cafe. Their *quiet* dinner at Magic Cafe.

They sat on the swing while Harry slowly pushed them back and forth, neither one of them wanting to address the obvious, she was leaving in the morning. Her heart clutched in her chest and her breaths seemed to be taking a lot of effort. The world was smothering her right now.

"Sams."

"Hm?"

"I wish things could be different." Harry's voice was low and rumbly.

She loved the sound of his voice.

"We could try the long distance relationship thing." Harry's voice didn't sound very sold on the idea.

"I'm not sure there's any point to that. The end would be the same. I can't leave my father's company. I can't. He'd be so disappointed. I can't hurt him like that. And I think today's lunch with my parents was just legal talk. I was silly to think it was anything different."

"I'm sorry."

"Sometimes life just doesn't give us what we hope for."

Harry tightened his arm around her shoulders. "I wish—"

"I know, Harry. I know."

"It's getting late and you have an early flight. I should probably go."

She didn't want him to go. She wanted to sit, with his arm around her shoulder, until dawn. But, she just nodded in agreement with him instead.

He pushed off the swing and pulled her to her feet. His strong arms wrapped around her, and he rested his head on hers. She threaded her arms around him and clung tightly. They stood that way for long minutes. Her heart cracked into tiny pieces, shattered with loss.

He pulled back and tilted her chin up. He leaned down and gave her a long, tender kiss, then pulled away. "I am glad you came back. I am glad we had this time together. I want only the best for you." He brushed a hand along the side of her face. "Goodbye, Sams."

She couldn't even choke out a goodbye. She reached up to cover the warm trail where his hand had just touch her. He turned and slowly walked away without turning back to glance at her. Not even once.

The cold night air descended on her, stifling her, freezing her, taunting her with thoughts of long, lonely nights ahead.

"Harry, I love you." She whispered into the night.

CHAPTER 26

"Samantha, did you hear me?" Sammy's father looked across the conference table at her. Out the window behind him, Chicago was showcasing one of its heavy, wet spring snowfalls.

"What? I... uh... I guess I missed it. What did you say?"

"Are you okay? Your mind seems elsewhere these days." Her father frowned.

"I'm sorry. You're right. I need to get my head back into the game. You were talking about a new account?" Sammy picked up her pen and opened her notebook, ready to take down anything her father said, anything to keep busy.

Her father sat and looked at her. Her father

looked amazingly relaxed today. The other day when she'd walked past his office, she swore she heard him whistling.

Glad someone was having a good time.

Her father interrupted her thoughts. "You're thinking about that young man, aren't you?"

"No." She sighed. "Well, a bit."

"I thought so." Her father picked up a sheet of paper in front of him and changed the subject. "Okay, let's see if we can come up with some ideas for this sporting goods campaign."

Sammy scribbled notes while she and her father bounced around ideas. Lots of notes. She'd go back to her office and carefully type them up when they were finished. With any luck, it would take her until late evening to do all that. Then she'd have that much less time in her cold, lonely apartment.

Sammy had managed to keep busy at the office until seven that evening. She'd wrapped up against the cold and walked the two blocks to her apartment. Her father didn't like her walking home at night by herself, but she wanted to feel the cold air, fight through the snow, battle *something* and feel like she was winning.

She changed into flannel jammies and a sweatshirt after she got home. After rummaging in the fridge, she pulled out some cheese and settled on cheese and crackers and a few slices of apple for dinner.

What she really wanted was blackened grouper.

At Magic Cafe.

With Harry.

Was this ever going to get easier? She missed him with every fiber of her being. His smile, his arms around her, his kiss. She missed just talking to him. She missed the sound of his voice. Her heart tightened.

She'd picked up the phone a hundred times to call him on lonely nights like this, but what would that help? It would just make it that much harder to get over him. She'd thought that he might call her, but he'd probably come to the same conclusion she had. There was really no point.

She walked to the window, stood with a glass of wine in her hand, and watched the wet snowflakes blanket the city.

Harry stood at Lighthouse Point. The days were getting warmer as the winter faded. Soon the snowbirds would all be gone back up North and it would be time to get ready for the summer season. More families came down this summer, versus retired couples in the winter. He'd almost finished Bellemire for Rose. She'd be back on the island soon, too.

The early spring sunshine warmed his skin as he sat on the beach, staring at the waves. He missed Sammy. Most days were hard without her. Some days were better than others. He was missing Sammy acutely today. Why he thought coming to Lighthouse Point would make him feel better was beyond him.

If he closed his eyes, he could almost imagine Sammy here with him, whirling and twirling in that carefree way she had. His heart squeezed and he curled his fists around two handfuls of sand. He let the sand slowly filter through his fingers until one lone shell remained on his palm. A perfect pink shell, with delicate sculpted edges.

Before he could stop himself or think about how crazy he was, he jumped up and raced across the sand. He stood at the water's edge and closed his eyes.

"I wish Sammy would come back to me."

He opened his eyes and threw the shell as far out into the sea as he could.

He looked both directions to see if anyone had seen his foolishness. But maybe, just maybe, there was some truth to the legend of Lighthouse Point. Maybe wishes made at the point do come true.

CHAPTER 27

"Go pack your bags." Sammy looked up as her father entered her office. "We're headed out."

"Where to?" Sammy wouldn't mind a break for the tedious routine her life had become. A lonely, tedious routine.

"Adriana recommended us to another small retail chain in Sarasota. Trendy house decor. We're scheduled to meet with them tomorrow to hear what they want. I've made all the travel arrangements."

Sammy swallowed. She wasn't sure if she was ready to be that close to Belle Island.

"Oh, and since we had such a good time on Belle Island, I got us a place to stay there."

Sammy's eyes widened. "I… it would probably be more convenient to stay at the Hamilton in Sarasota, wouldn't it?"

"Probably, but you could use a break. You've been moping around for weeks. The sunshine will do you good. I hear they're having low eighty degree weather. Much nicer than March weather in Chicago, don't you think? Flight leaves in four hours. I'll have my driver pick you up."

Sammy gripped her notebook. She wasn't ready for this. Her father had caught her off guard.

"Oh, and Samantha?" Her father paused and turned back in the doorway. "Your mother is coming with us."

Sammy dropped her notebook on the desk and watched as it slid off and crashed on the floor.

Sammy spent the whole flight trying to make small talk with her parents. Her mother sat in the middle seat next to her father. Her unusually jovial father. Her mother laughed. Often.

"Samantha, I hope you're okay with me joining you on the trip. I had such a great time on the island and when your father invited me to join you, well, I couldn't resist."

"No, I'm glad you're going. It was lucky you happened to be in Chicago." Why had her mother been in Chicago?

"Oh, I've been staying in Chicago for... a while."

"You have?" Sammy leaned forward and looked from her mother to her father.

"We thought it best if we just kept that to ourselves for a bit. We're not really sure where things are going, but I asked your mother to come to Chicago. We've been... dating, I guess you'd call it."

Sammy didn't think the day could get more surprising. "You, what?"

"Well, your father and I are just getting to know each other again." Her mother's eyes sparkled.

Sammy turned and looked out the plane's window at the clouds stacked in fluffy white columns. Her mother and her father. Dating. She rubbed her temples. She needed time to think, everything was happening so quickly.

The plane landed and they were all soon headed to Belle Island. The driver took them past Belle Island Inn. "We're not staying at the inn?" Sammy's forehead creased in a frown.

"Ah, not exactly." Her father grinned.

Grinned. It was a full out grin.

They pulled in front of a cute cottage on Lighthouse Point. "Oh, you rented a cottage." Sammy relaxed. Then sat up straight. Wait? The three of them were going to stay in the cottage together?

She slowly opened her car door and climbed out of the car. Her father walked quickly to the cottage and opened the door. She followed her mother inside.

"Oh, it's lovely, Phillip." Her mother moved further into the cottage.

Sunshine spilled through the windows that reached floor to ceiling across the ocean side of the cottage. A nice-sized kitchen with stainless appliances was separated from the great room by only a cherry island with four comfortable-looking barstools.

"It's really nice, Dad." Sammy looked around in appreciation. It was just the kind of cottage she loved.

"Three bedrooms, three baths. And a deck that wraps around the side of the cottage." Her father grinned again. *Grinned.* He held out the key. "Your mother and I are staying at the inn." He dropped the key into her hand.

"What? You're not staying here?"

"We'll see you later, dear." Her mother smiled

conspiratorially at her dad.

"I—" Sammy tried to speak.

"The driver will be here at nine in the morning to pick you up. We'll go to the meeting in Sarasota. Oh, and I had the kitchen stocked for you."

"Dad, I—"

"Oh, and by the way. The cottage is yours. You own it. I put it in your name."

Sammy collapsed onto one of those comfortable-looking barstools. "What are you talking about? Why?"

"Well, I think you like visiting here. Thought you'd like a place to stay when you do." There was that grin on her dad's face again.

Even her mother was grinning.

She was surrounded by grins in a world that was spinning out of control. "Dad, I don't understand. I can't accept this."

"Sure, you can, honey." Her mother crossed over to stand by her dad.

"Your mother and I have plans this evening. I'll see you in the morning, honey."

Her mother rested her hand on her father's arm, and with that, her parents disappeared out the door. Sammy looked down at the key clutched tightly in her hand.

Sammy stood and spun around slowly, taking in

the simple, coastal decor of the cottage. She crossed to the floor-to-ceiling sliding doors and threw them open. The warm sea breeze rushed over her.

The familiar view of the ocean soothed her jangled nerves. *Kind of.*

Now what?

Harry looked up from his desk to see Sammy's father standing in the doorway to his office. "Sir." Harry stood.

"Harry, I need you to do me a favor."

"Of course. What can I do for you?" What could *he* do for Sammy's father?

"I need you to go to Lighthouse Point."

"What?" Harry frowned.

"Go to Lighthouse Point, then walk back to where the cottages start. Count back four cottages. A green cottage. Well, Shelly says it's mint colored, you know how women are about colors."

"Sir?"

"And call me, Phillip, not Sir."

"I—"

"Samantha is at the cottage. I think you two should talk."

"Sammy is here?"

"She is. And I'm thinking there is something going on between you two. Something strong and real. Shelly thinks it's been going on for over twenty years. Seems a bit silly to throw that away, doesn't it?

"I—"

"You have to take risks in life if you want to chase your dreams."

"I—"

Sammy's dad wasn't letting Harry get in any words to stop the tidal wave of surprises.

"And, another thing. She's under some mistaken impression that she has to be in Chicago to help me run my business. As I said, it's a mistaken notion. There are video calls, planes that can take her back to Chicago when needed, and oh, email and things like that. We could open a satellite office in Tampa or Sarasota. Sometimes you've got to think out of the box in my business." Mr. Thompson—*Phillip*—grinned. "And you tell her I said so."

"I… I sure will." Harry's heart thundered and his pulse raced. Sammy was here. *Here*.

"So you'll get this all sorted out?" Sammy's father said it more of a command than a question.

"I'll try my hardest."

"Oh, and son?"

"Yes, sir… I mean, Phillip."

245

"You take care of her."

"I will. I promise."

Sammy's father left the office and Harry snatched the keys to the van. He was going to do exactly what Mr. Thompson—Phillip—how long would it take to get used to calling him that? Anyway, he was going to do exactly what the man said. He was going to get things all sorted out with Sammy. Right now. Before anything else crazy could get between them.

Sammy sat on the deck, watching the sunset. She couldn't decide if she should call Harry. What would change? She would still be going back to Chicago and he'd still be here. But how could she stay away from him while she was here? And why had her father put her in this position? She analyzed the day from each and every angle.

A lone man jogged down the beach towards the cottage. Even though she couldn't see him clearly yet in the distance, she knew, just *knew*, it was Harry.

She jumped up from her chair and raced onto the beach. The sand tugged at her feet as she sped across the distance. As she got closer—and yes it was Harry, *she'd known it, felt it*—he upped his pace and raced towards her.

She jumped into this arms and he caught her close. "Sams." Harry buried his face in her hair.

"Oh, Harry. I've missed you so much."

Harry spun around with her in his arms. "You have no idea, Sams. I was going crazy without you."

He set her down and kissed her gently on the lips. She sighed, she couldn't help herself. He pulled away. "Sammy, we need to talk."

"But—"

Harry touched his finger to her lips. "Let me talk first. I have a message from your father."

"My dad? How—"

Harry cocked his head and eyed her and she stopped with the questions.

"He says you have a mistaken notion about your job. His exact words were that in your business you have to think out of the box. He said you could work from here. Fly back when you need to. He said something about opening a satellite office here."

"He…" This time Harry didn't have to stop her. She had no words. Suddenly laughter spilled out of her and she threw her arms wide and whirled around on the beach.

Harry's laugh filled the air around her. "I've missed your swirling dance, Sams."

She hurried back towards him and threw herself in his arms. He hugged her tightly against him, but then suddenly stepped away.

"One more thing."

She looked up into his eyes questioningly. "What's the one more thing?"

"Two things, actually."

"One, I love you, Sams."

"Oh." The sound whooshed from her mouth and her heart pounded. "I love you too. I have for forever it seems."

"Ha, you love me, too. I knew it." Harry grinned. "Anyway, I said there were two things."

"What's the second thing?" She eyed him, her heart brimming with joy.

Harry dropped to one knee. "I know you'll need to time think about it. I know you take time with decisions. Take as long as you want. But... will you marry me, Sams?"

"Oh, Harry. Yes. Yes, I'll marry you." She said it with no hesitation, sure of her decision in an instant.

Harry stood, a trace of tears hiding in the corners of his eyes. He wrapped his arms around her and everything in her world fell perfectly into place.

CHAPTER 28

A week later Sammy stood on the beach in front of Magic Cafe. As the sun set in the distance, Sammy and Harry repeated their vows. He walked her down the aisle after the ceremony and held her hand tightly in his.

They went onto the deck at Magic Cafe where they'd reserved a few tables for a reception. Jamie and Cindy were there, along with Mary, Dorothy, Adam and Susan. Julie had made them a small wedding cake with one lone shell as a cake topper. Harry told everyone he saw about his wish on Lighthouse Point.

Sammy looked over at where her parents were standing, their heads close together. Her mother smiled at something her dad said. Her father held her mother's hand in his.

She couldn't imagine a more perfect wedding, a more perfect day.

"Sams?" Harry looked down at her and smiled that just-for-her smile.

"What?" She smiled back at him and reached out to touch his face.

"Two things."

"Again with the two things." She laughed.

"One, I love you."

"I like that that's always number one."

"And two." He covered her hand with his. "Never doubt the power of a wish made at Lighthouse Point."

THANK YOU for reading my story. I hope you enjoyed it. Sign up for my newsletter to be updated with information on new releases, promotions, and give-aways. The signup is at my website, kaycorrell.com.

Reviews help other readers find new books. I always appreciate when my readers take time to leave an honest review.

I love to hear from my readers. Feel free to contact me at authorcontact@kaycorrell.com

COMFORT CROSSING ~ THE SERIES

The Shop on Main - Book One

The Memory Box - Book Two

The Christmas Cottage - A Holiday Novella (Book 2.5)

The Letter - Book Three

The Christmas Scarf - A Holiday Novella (Book 3.5)

The Magnolia Cafe - Book Four

The Unexpected Wedding - Book Five

The Wedding in the Grove (crossover short story between series - Josephine and Paul from The Letter.)

LIGHTHOUSE POINT ~ THE SERIES

Wish Upon a Shell - Book One

Wedding on the Beach - Book Two

Love at the Lighthouse - Book Three

Cottage near the Point - Book Four

Return to the Island - Book Five

INDIGO BAY ~ a multi-author series of sweet romance

Sweet Sunrise - Book Three

Sweet Holiday Memories - A short holiday story

Sweet Starlight - Book Nine

ABOUT THE AUTHOR

Kay writes sweet, heartwarming stories that are a cross between women's fiction and contemporary romance. She is known for her charming small towns, quirky townsfolk, and enduring strong friendships between the women in her books.

Kay lives in the Midwest of the U.S. and can often be found out and about with her camera, taking a myriad of photographs which she likes to incorporate into her book covers. When not lost in her writing or photography, she can be found spending time with her ever-supportive husband, knitting, working in her garden, or playing with her puppies—two cavaliers and one naughty but adorable Australian shepherd. Kay and her husband also love to travel. When it comes to vacation time, she is torn between a nice trip to the beach or the mountains—but the mountains only get considered in the summer—she swears she's allergic to snow.

Learn more about Kay and her books at
kaycorrell.com

While you're there, sign up for her newsletter to hear about new releases, sales, and giveaways.

WHERE TO FIND ME:
kaycorrell.com
authorcontact@kaycorrell.com

Join my Facebook Reader Group. We have lots of fun and you'll hear about sales and new releases first!
https://www.facebook.com/groups/KayCorrell/

,

Made in the USA
Coppell, TX
27 June 2020